'Visions'

To
Sandra
Best Wishes

[signature]

**I was born when you kissed me
I lived while you loved me
I died when you left me**

Herbert Edgar

'Visions'
'I was born when you kissed me'

Herbert Edgar

VIKI Books
Inverness. Florida

Revised edition May 1995

Library of Congress Catalog Card Number: 95-60756

Visions : a novel by Herbert Edgar

ISBN 0-9640363-3-9

Published in the United States by: Viki Books
Inverness
Florida 34451-1228

Printed in the U.S.A.   --   First edition: February 1994
Revised edition: May 1995

Book design by Geoffrey Terry

'Visions'

Valerie awoke, opened her eyes and decided it must still be dark of night; however, the regular movement of traffic on the secondary road at the front of the building made her think again. How could it be so dark?

She swung her feet over the side of the bed, made the few steps across to the window, fumbled for the drapes and opened them; as she did so a cold chill ran down her spine.

There was no one else in the apartment with whom to express the fear she felt, so she stumbled across the room and grabbed the telephone. Having no idea of time she decided to call her mother, who was always home. What a blessing there was the memory button. The number rang only twice before the soothing voice of her mother.

"Hello."

How does one say I think I have just gone blind, she thought, and to one's mother?

That, in fact, was the only thing to say and having made that terrible statement she burst into tears, her legs gave way and she collapsed to the floor, trembling and desperate.

It seemed like only moments and it seemed like hours before she heard the turn of the key in the lock.

Her mother ran to where her daughter lay sobbing and as she knelt beside her became conscious of the tears that began to run down her own face.

"Come, my dear, I will help you dress. We must go to the hospital immediately and for the moment hope and pray that whatever has happened may just as easily reverse. Come, come quickly."

She guided her to the bathroom, helped her to prepare and very soon they were hurrying, as best they could under the new circumstances, down to the foyer of the apartment block, where the taxi was already waiting,

It was a little after 9:30 a.m. and as usual the traffic was very heavy as they began their journey. Valerie's mother outlined the situation to the taxi driver who took exceptional steps to expedite their passage, changing lanes, crossing red lights and sounding his horn incessantly to try to clear the way. For once he would have been happy to be stopped by a police patrol, who could then have cleared a passage for them. He cursed silently to himself that, as usual, when you need them they are not there.

Every stop, every deceleration amplified the nervous strain that now affected the three occupants of the vehicle. Whatever speed the taxi achieved, it could not be fast enough to satisfy the anxious desire of the mother and daughter to hear the diagnosis.

Once at the hospital they made their way to the emergency room and nervously the mother blurted out the shocking situation. The sister was not qualified to offer an opinion, nor was she prepared to conjecture as to a cause or possible cure for Valerie's condition.

They were frustratingly obliged to complete the documentation, each question an obstacle, each moment an age.

Finally the doctor came. He spoke gently and calmly, forcing upon them a similar reaction.

Soon they would know. The doctor must be given absolute quiet to follow his procedures; whatever he found should be based upon careful analysis of the symptoms, not diverted by nervous chatter.

Following his examination, the doctor declared that he was not in a position to give a firm diagnosis. It would be necessary for her to be seen by a specialist. Fortunately, there was one in the building and he was summoned.

There was a further half-hour of nervous anticipation.

When the specialist did arrive he was an understanding man and appreciated the psychological implications of the circumstances outlined to him by the doctor who had examined her previously.

He followed his procedures scrupulously and finally presented his diagnosis.

The technical medical explanation was beyond their comprehension, nevertheless, the general position was quite clear. The blindness could last hours, days, months or even years.

The *fait accompli* that, today, made a frightening situation terrifying.

ONE

Twenty minutes into the journey Valerie realized that the train was running out of control.

She heard no screams or cries for help, suggesting that the compartment in which she was travelling carried no other passengers; invariably the situation, from her previous experience of that route.

She stood, held the handrail and fumbled for the emergency lever, which to her surprise she found quite quickly. With her right hand she took a firm hold of the handle and whilst pulling down grabbed her wrist with the other hand, effectively doubling the force. The handle dropped to the stop position and she braced herself for the jolt as the emergency brake was applied. But there was no jolt, there was no reduction in the speed of the runaway train. In fact the speed continued to increase as did the instability.

Valerie decided she must get as far to the rear of the train as possible, in anticipation of a certain, massive impact.

Little by little she hauled herself along the corridor, fighting the motion of the train and stabilizing herself with anything her hands found.

Then there was something soft. Her hand had alighted upon the arm of someone, someone who made no movement and said nothing. How could it be? "Who is there?" she tentatively inquired.

Silence, a silence that only served to intensify the already terrifying situation.

Roberto had been watching her in her struggle. She had long auburn hair, tossed by the erratic movements of the train. Her thin summer dress, now clinging, now billowing, had the effect of enhancing her slim, gracious form.

She was the girl from his dreams.

For two years, two or three times a week he had dreamed of this girl; there was no doubt that it was she. They had made love, glorious passionate love and yet now she was beside him he realized that he didn't even know her name.

By her movements and the white cane she carried he saw that she was blind. What had happened to her? In his dreams she had not been so.

He decided not to respond. She loved him as much as he loved her. Once he took her in his arms she would know him. It would be a wonderful surprise and in their last moments of life they would be together.

It was a hopeless situation in which they now found themselves and his desire to make love to her once more before they both surely died became so intense that he was almost oblivious to their circumstances.

Before she could release her grip on his arm he had taken a firm hold of her, encircling her waist with one arm while his other hand explored rapidly all those beautiful and forbidden places.

In an instant he pulled her to the floor. Valerie knew it was useless to scream, there was no one to hear her. Her energy must be conserved for some positive action.

She still had hold of her white stick. That was her lifeline and held her only hope. With her thumb she pushed the knob on top of the stick and the outer casing slipped away, exposing a deadly blade which, without delay, she thrust forward aiming to disable that part that coveted her most.

Her aim, guided by that instinct that blind people possess, was good, she came very close and he screamed in agony as the four-inch, razor-sharp, double-sided knife sunk deep into the flesh of the inside of his leg. She retained her hold and with all the power she could muster forced in a sideways motion. The flesh of the muscle severed and blood gushed.

He released his grip of her, rolled onto his side, then was instantly thrown back on top of her by the motion of the train.

She still held the deadly blade. Now her grip would be tested, because with one hand he grabbed her wrist and forced her arm back against the edge of the seat.

"Why?" he cried. "Do you not know me?"

She screamed as he applied as much pressure as he could.

By now there was a large pool of blood and the force he was applying was dependent on his right knee, which suddenly slipped in the red plasma. At the same moment the train left the track and immediately rolled on to one side, an action that sent him slithering in his own blood, impacting him against the door.

The momentum continued. The carriage had disengaged from the others and sped down the embankment like some mad bull.

Valerie succeeded in maintaining her grip on the blade while her other hand took a firm hold on the seat. She hauled herself upward until she was on the side of the seat, at which moment the carriage arrived at the base of the embankment, rolled once more, this time to the inverted position and came to a violent stop, as the front impacted a huge rock that protruded from the side of the mountain.

She, with the final, rapid, erratic jerk, was thrown against the wall of the carriage, her head receiving a severe blow.

For a moment she was stunned but as she regained her senses, the whole scene began to open up to her. She saw with perfect clarity all the detail of her surroundings during the previous minutes.

The return of her sight at that moment did not give her the opportunity to contemplate the event, nor to utter her thanks to God for the return of that wonderful gift that had been denied her for one terrible year. The situation in which she now found herself dictated swift, calm action.

Her concern was for the man who had assaulted her, who had defied the unwritten law of those who are sighted to protect and assist those less fortunate, the cruel, evil being who, in the interest of his own lust, had rendered further terror to a helpless fellow traveller.

It was an opportune moment that concluded a period of permanent night for her. The positive result of the train crash was that now she would be able to see her assailant. She felt her body tense in anticipation of a potential further encounter.

She glanced to where he lay still and moaning, his own blood dripping onto him from the floor, now above. Perhaps there would be no further encounter.

Her first instinct was to get as far away from him as possible; however, for the outrageous act he had perpetrated upon her, he should be punished. He should be arrested, handcuffed, have chains fixed to his ankles and taken to face the humiliation, not only of an attempted rape but also be exposed before the courts and the public for the circumstances of that attempt.

To that end she reconsidered her next move.

As she began to think logically the cocktail of fear, desperation and anger within her began to subside, her breathing lessened in intensity and the pounding from her heart, that had shaken her whole body, faded.

She glanced at him once more. The pool of blood was such, she realized the possibility she had severed an artery. He should not die, that would constitute primitive, angry revenge. The courts existed to deal with such matters. Justice was not perfect but she was confident he would receive his just reward.

Slowly she moved toward him.

"Please help me," he begged, still in a state of disbelief. Why had she done it? Perhaps he *had* confused a dream with reality. It had all been so real, exactly as in the dream; he had been so sure. Now, in retrospect, he realized that she had not known him. His passionate belief that they had finally found one another had been misguided. What had he done?

In her previous blind state she had imagined an ugly, maybe slightly obese, middle-aged man. Almost bald, palefaced, badly shaven with perhaps a boil on his nose. Now with her clarity of mind and vision she saw that he was very handsome, in his early thirties and elegantly dressed, to the extent of a red rose in his lapel. His complexion suggested Mediterranean, probably Italian. His face was very distinctive with bold features and a carefully trimmed moustache.

"No, please," he implored, thinking that the knife she had retained so tenaciously and now moving toward him once more, was intended to put an end to his miserable life. She made no comment, simply cut a strip of material from his shirt, quickly made a tourniquet and tightened it around his thigh.

He needed a blood transfusion, urgently. The rapid pumping was now reduced but still his body was draining. She cut a further strip of material from his shirt, then held the knife to his throat.

"Hold out your hands." He had no strength to argue or fight and did as instructed. She utilized the strip of material to bind his wrists tightly. Then with yet another strip she anchored him firmly to the luggage rack.

The concave shape of the inside of the carriage roof presented a substantial obstacle as she tried to make her way to the door. Once there she was faced with a greater problem. In the inverted position the door became extremely heavy. After several unsuccessful attempts to open it she finally decided to exit via the window. By that method she succeeded in leaving the ambiance of terror.

In sharp contrast to her previous circumstances, the day was beautiful. It was about 3 p.m. The sun shone soft and warm and the only sound was that of a skylark circling high above. A gentle breeze seemed oblivious to the twisted masses of metal scattered along the embankment, and the carriage, that had been her prison, looked ridiculous with its wheels trying to make contact with the sky.

First she ran to the front of the carriage and scrambled up the rock that had acted as a brake. Beyond the rock was nothing, just a sheer drop of perhaps three or four thousand feet to the valley below. There, deep in the distance, it was just possible to make out the buildings of the village, surrounded by a patchwork quilt of colour defining the fields and pine forests.

Her mind seemed to flip-flop between the joy of the passage of light through the lenses of her eyes to the retina, where minute electrical impulses conveyed the millions of bits of information to her brain, which drank in the beauty like a perfect wine, then to the brutal reality of the situation and the image of that wicked man clear in her mind, almost the first matter to be transmitted in detail to her brain for a whole year.

It occurred to her that perhaps the train carried a telephone in the guards' compartment and with that thought in mind she clambered up the embankment to where she expected to find the rest of the train.

On arrival at the top she stood in the middle of the track and scanned slowly over a 360° arc. There were no other carriages, nor the engine to be seen. Evidently the rest of the train had not been arrested by a rock, as in the case of the carriage in which she had been travelling, and had plunged to the valley below.

She had never actually seen the mountain nor any part of the area before. She had been living there for the past eight months, but before that time had never visited the area at all. Even so she had travelled the route many times and had a picture in her mind created from sound and time.

There remained still approximately twenty-five minutes of journey to the valley, the only other stop being a service facility of the railway company.

She began to contemplate having to make the journey by foot, when there came the unmistakable sound of a helicopter, suggesting that there was a rescue operation already underway.

Perhaps thirty minutes had elapsed from the moment of impact. Presumably the other carriages plunging into the valley had been observed by someone, accounting for the rapid instigation of a search.

Apparently the pilot had seen her and began to descend. She ran back to the carriage, climbed in and without understanding her own actions cut loose the strips of material securing the man and binding his hands. He now lay unconscious.

She quickly located the casing of her white stick and slid the blade back into place, then ran outside.

The helicopter had alighted beside the track and the pilot was already making his way to the carriage. She met him and confirmed there had been just two survivors.

They climbed inside the carriage and she led him to where the other passenger lay, his face now quite white. The pilot knelt beside the motionless figure, checked the pulse in his neck and observed that there was no time to go for a stretcher.

"This man will soon die. We must get him to the hospital. It's a ten minute flight from here."

Fortunately the pilot was a well-built man and succeeded in lifting the lifeless figure onto his shoulder. Then he made his way along the upturned carriage to the door which he managed to open, having first relieved himself of his burden. Valerie jumped down first and was able to be of some help in lowering the injured man to the ground. Soon the pilot was struggling up the embankment, she behind pushing him with all her force.

Finally they arrived at the helicopter and within a couple of minutes were airborne.

The flight to the hospital took ten minutes, as the pilot had estimated. On touchdown two nurses were already waiting with a stretcher and rushed the lifeless figure directly into the operating theatre.

Valerie turned to the pilot and thanked him for what he had done. He replied, "I hope your husband will be OK," then shook her hand, ran to the helicopter and took off.

A group of people had gathered. Some from newspapers began to fire questions at her which she felt incapable of answering, feeling very confused. Shortly a police officer stepped in front of the other inquisitors and calmly enquired how she felt. She responded that she felt reasonably well, under the circumstances.

He asked for her personal details, which she gave him, then for those of her husband, "He is not my husband, we are just friends," she replied.

The statement issued from her mouth as though from another. What was happening to her? However, having made that statement she felt obliged to continue in the same vein.

Before the police officer could continue with his questioning the surgeon appeared and beckoned to her. She excused herself and moved quickly, expecting the worst.

"We have a problem which you may have anticipated. Your husband requires a transfusion; however, as you are of course aware, he has a very rare blood group and we have not succeeded in locating the necessary plasma."

"He is not my husband, we are just friends." She repeated the same enigmatic statement, "What is his blood group?"

The surgeon's reply highlighted a remarkable coincidence.

"That is also my blood group. You may take what you need from me, just tell me what I must do."

"You have suffered a trauma yourself. Do you feel up to it?" the surgeon replied.

"Yes, I am fine. Let's hurry."

He led her into the operating theatre and the nurse prepared her.

This was an extraordinary situation, after the despicable way in which he had used her she was now saving his life.

Her blood would soon be circulating in his body. His black heart would share the same thin red ribbon that had previously tried and tried to massage her eyes into life.

She lay still for a few moments, then her eyelids began to feel heavy and slowly, once more, closed off the light to her eyes. The tension, the fright, the nervous exhaustion had all taken their toll upon her natural strength and it would be necessary to take the maximum amount of blood to help replenish that lost by her 'friend'.

How many hours she had lain, she could not determine. Her mind had rebelled and closed all channels of operation.

When she did open her eyes she was not at all surprised that no light entered, though that sensation was only very momentary. The cold chill she had experienced one year ago travelled up her spine once more. Had it all been a dream? Had she regained her sight for that brief moment?

Her experienced fingers delicately stroked the face of her watch, 2 a.m. That was it, everything she thought she had experienced had been a nightmare with a touch of wonder, the temporary return of her sight.

She mentally dismissed the horror aspect and allowed the passage through her mind of the visions she had revelled in. It had all been so clear. She closed her eyes again hoping to recapture the joy of once more having her sight.

Try though she may she could not conjure up any of the scenes of beauty she was so sure she had witnessed. Over and over again she felt the stranger throwing her to the floor, she felt the knife enter his flesh, then she felt the sudden arresting of the carriage and emitted a scream.

The door opened and the light was switched on.

"Are you all right?" a female voice enquired.

Again her eyes opened. It was reality. She had recovered her sight.

"Yes, I had a nightmare. Nurse, would you please turn off the light for a moment."

"Of course."

"And now close the door."

"OK, but why?"

When she awoke earlier, obviously the light was off and the door closed. Here was the identical situation, the room was pitch black.

"You may switch on the light again now. I would like to telephone my mother and tell her that I am all right."

"Your mother is here, she learned of the accident and came immediately. She has been waiting, not wishing to disturb you. By the way I am sure you will be pleased to know that your husband is off the danger list. The cut on the inside of his leg is quite serious and he will not walk for a very long time; nevertheless the surgeon believes he will recover fully in time."

"I don't know why everyone insists on speaking of him as my husband. He is not my husband." Before she could continue, she remembered what she had said to the policeman and the helicopter pilot, "He is just a friend," she added. Yet another time repeating the same phrase.

"Do you feel up to seeing your mother now?"

"Yes, please send her in and leave the light on."

The nurse left the room.

During the next few moments Valerie would be obliged to devise a story for her mother. Not wishing to worry her with the attempted rape, she decided, for the moment, to concentrate on the miracle of the return of her sight and hope that questions regarding the stranger would not arise.

"Valerie, my poor darling, I have been hearing the most amazing things. Tell me first, how are you?"

"Mother, your coat is a very nice colour and I like your hat."

A powerful silence resounded. The statement came as a great shock to her mother who had lived with her daughter's blindness long enough that she recognized the significance of what she heard. She felt both overjoyed and weak at the knees. Sitting on the bed to stabilize herself she calmly enquired, "Can it be? Have you recovered your sight?"

"Yes, mother. In the train crash I received a severe blow to the head and when I opened my eyes I saw as clearly as I had the day before that awful Friday."

"Darling, I am so happy. When I heard the news of the train crash I thought I had lost you. Now I must be grateful that you were a passenger on that train. The surgeon told me you appear to have come through unscathed, but you must be very weak. Anyone would be weak after such a traumatic experience and then to give blood. I am so curious to know of your relationship with Roberto Grassina."

"Mother, forgive me, I would like to sleep now. We can speak in the morning. You go home and when they release me I will take a taxi. Then we can talk about everything. I will call you when I'm about to leave."

"All right, dear, don't worry about anything, just get as much sleep as you can. There is no need to hurry home, the important thing is that you get all the rest you need. Goodbye, dear, I will see you soon."

"Goodbye, mother."

The door closed and once more Valerie was alone with her thoughts. She really was tired, even so it was important to prepare a story for her mother. The situation was very delicate and required very careful consideration. For the next two hours she went over and over the circumstances in her mind, then, once again, sleep overcame her.

The following morning she awoke at nine and realized she had still not arrived at a feasible story. Her mouth was very dry and she turned to ring the bell for the nurse, then caught her breath when, as she turned to reach for the bell, she saw the stranger sitting in a wheelchair beside her bed still looking very pale. He wore a vermilion silk dressing gown, though the elegance was lost by the protrusion of one leg in a large plaster cast, thrusting directly forward and resting on the small platform of the wheelchair.

He observed her reaction which also made it quite clear to him that she had her sight. Even so there was no sign of recognition in her beautiful eyes.

She did *not* know him.

"Excuse my forwardness, but I believed you to be blind," he observed, "now I see that you are not."

He was brazen. Presumably he felt confident because, so far, she had not denounced him and had saved his life by the donation of her blood.

"I want you to know immediately that my concern for your life was to ensure that you stand trial for what you did before the final crash of the carriage."

"It is necessary that we speak. First please permit me to introduce myself. My name is Roberto Grassina. Maybe you have heard of my father, Baron Ernesto Grassina." He handed her a card which she declined to accept, leaving it on the bedside table.

"Had you been a drug addict or a drunken sailor, I might not have been surprised at your action, but someone in your position, with your father so respected and an advocate of corporal punishment, devoted to discipline and honor. You must be insane, unable to distinguish between good and evil."

"Please, I beg you to permit me to explain the circumstances and try, with me, to understand what happened."

"I see no point. There is nothing you could say that would in any way affect my intention to see you before a judge. You must never again be permitted to have the possibility of arriving in a situation where you might behave in a similar manner. Please leave me. You will have ample opportunity to describe the circumstances in court".

As she uttered the words she had the incredible sensation that she did not want him to leave. How could she feel so about someone who had tried to rape her?

He turned the wheelchair and began to move toward the door, his mind still in a turmoil. Obviously it really was only a dream. She didn't know him. It was not just that she had been blind on the train.

"One moment, tell me one thing. You must have your choice of women, are you starved of love? Do you get your pleasure by the infliction of pain and terror on others? Are you a sadist?"

"Valerie, that is your name, I believe. Like you I have experienced blindness, in fact I was born blind. Then a miracle occurred. Just about one year ago, I awoke one morning to the full glory of the world. I was thirty-two years old. Someone born sighted could not possibly imagine the shock of suddenly gaining ones' sight so late in life."

"What you tell me now only makes the situation worse. You knew how helpless I was and how I depended on others to guide me through my day. You did not have to imagine what was in my mind, you knew, and still had no mercy."

"There is one other very important fact that I implore you to allow me to relate. For about two years I had the same repeated dream. The extraordinary thing is that images appeared in my mind before I had ever experienced the joy of seeing. Those images continued up until a few days ago, the same scene each time. I stood with my hand on a railing watching as a beautiful girl came toward me. We knew each other, we were lovers who had been parted for a long time, each of us hungry for the other. As the girl arrived beside me, the desire exploded within me, I grasped her with an arm around her waist and we began to make passionate love."

Valerie was touched by his sincere expression and found herself beginning to believe what she heard. He continued,

"That dream became reality yesterday afternoon on the train when I saw you walking toward me. You were the image of the girl in my dream. As you reached me and placed your hand on my arm, that same passion filled me, my blood surged within me and I was on fire with desire. I didn't consider for a moment that we were unknown to each other. We belonged to each other. You cannot imagine my shock when I felt the knife enter my leg. At first I thought perhaps I had moved against some protruding metal object. When I realized what was happening, for me it was the woman I loved, the woman who loved me turning on me like an angry beast."

"I refuse to listen to this feeble attempt to cover your base action. There is nothing you can say, no fiction you can invent that will save you from the course of the law."

"What I have told you, I have already written in a book that is with my publisher. If you will just give me the opportunity, I will have my publisher bring the manuscript here and you will be able to read an exact description of yourself. There can be no doubt that it is you who appeared in my dreams. The book was begun while I was still blind, dictated to my sister. I could not possibly have seen you when I described a mirror image of you, to the extent of the dress you wore on the train and your beautiful hair tossed by the movement of the train."

"How can you imagine that I could believe what you are saying. If you had never been sighted it would be impossible for you to conjure up images of anything."

"What you say I would agree with had I not been the one to experience the dream. It became an obsession with me. I could not wait for night and sleep. When the dream arrived, as it did two or three times a week, I experienced the ultimate joy, a passion so intense a sighted person could not possibly comprehend. For me it was something normal. I was as an inhabitant of another world, believing that everyone had similar dreams. My instinctive sense of privacy, at first, prevented me from discussing the dream with anyone. Many times girls had spoken softly to me and used the excuse of helping me to touch me. Each time I rejected their advances. The girl in my dreams was the only one I desired."

"This book of yours, if it exists, what is the title?"

"It has an ambiguous title. It is called, 'Visions of a Blind Man.' Please give me the opportunity to defend myself to justify what, I realize now, became for you a horrible and terrifying experience. I will telephone my publisher, here, in front of you. He will bring the manuscript and you may read for yourself, then judge me, having before you the matter that gave me the confidence to act as I did."

"I cannot imagine that anything you can say or have written could possibly justify your actions; however, I will read what you have written. There is the telephone, make your call."

He made the telephone call and told her that the manuscript would arrive during the afternoon.

That having been done, they agreed to delay any further discussions until Valerie had read the manuscript. Then he left her alone.

An hour later the doctor attending Valerie called and suggested that it would be in order for her to stay with her mother for a couple of days to rest and recover from the terrible experience of the train crash. Yet again she avoided telling him what had transpired and what had caused her far more distress than the train crash, nor did she mention the miracle of the return of her sight.

On her way out of the hospital she left instructions at the reception desk that when the courier arrived with the manuscript, he should take it to her mother's address.

TWO

By the time the courier arrived at her mother's apartment, Valerie had concocted a story about having met Grassina at the Center for the Blind and that they were travelling on the train together at the time of the crash.

Her mother expressed surprise that he would send the manuscript of his book to someone he had met so casually. Valerie justified it by suggesting that it was because she had given her blood, an act that certainly saved his life and good enough reason that he would wish to make some generous gesture.

On the pretext of feeling tired Valerie retired to the spare bed that was always made up for her in the apartment. She took with her the manuscript.

"To help me relax," she told her mother.

The apartment was in a quiet cul-de-sac and the only sound to accompany her reading was that of the incessant chirping of the sparrows on the birch trees outside her window. It was about 4 p.m. when she began.

The more she read the more amazed she became. Not only was the story as he had described but it was evident that he was a man of great talent as an author and of considerable sensitivity and feeling as a man.

A sense of relief began to overtake her as she realized that the circumstances were not so simple and barbaric as they had at first appeared.

Reading the passages of passion so intimate and touching, she became aware that her body began to tingle and she felt a need for him. Common sense intervened and she skipped the more sensual passages.

The description of the girl with the apricot-coloured dress and auburn hair was so detailed that thinking logically it had to be that he had seen a photograph of her, or heard a description from someone.

She was not convinced. Maybe whilst she was at the Blind Center, during the preceding year, he had seen her and devised the excuse he was now using.

The gentle feelings that had begun to overtake her quickly gave way to anger once more. She grabbed the telephone and called the blind school; then, as the ringing tone commenced she hurriedly replaced the receiver. Her heart was beating fast and something inside was telling her she must see him again.

Valerie read on for a few moments, then slowly the lids of her eyes grew heavy and for the next nine hours she mentally departed from the apartment, experiencing a most extraordinary dream.

This time it was she who succumbed to the marvel of the creativity of a released mind, released from the constrictions of being awake.

She found herself in a stately hall, baroque, grand and formal. Around a huge antique table sat a group of dignitaries, evidently important delegates participating in a conference of some sort. Above their heads, on the wall, was a large banner on which was printed:

Slovak Peoples Democratic Union.

September 24th, 1993.

The dream was so realistic, it was as though she were watching the scene on a giant screen.

Once she awoke she was able to recapture every detail of the dream. One of the gentlemen at the conference was highlighted in her memory, a face she did not know but somehow felt to be that of the father of Roberto. Then she realized that she had heard no words, there were only people and movement.

Her head began to ache with the confusion; no longer could she rely wholly on common sense or intelligence. She was bursting with the need to speak to someone. Her mother was rational, level-headed and absolutely reliable; whatever Valerie told her was sacred. Even so she felt that the only person to speak to was Roberto. Who was he? She knew nothing about him.

She turned to the fly leaf of the manuscript, 'Visions of a Blind Man' by Robert Garden. He had used a nom de plume and there was no curriculum vita included.

Then she remembered the card he had handed her. She had refused it but once he left her room she had taken it from the night stand and placed it in her purse. It was there and in gold script, embossed upon the card, his name, Roberto Grassina, that she knew already. The only other thing that appeared on the card was his name once more, in braille, confirming that he had been blind.

Somehow looking at his name seemed to relax her. Again she began to experience the need to be near him, to talk to him. That was not possible; she must eradicate those thoughts from her mind.

Now the old Valerie began to take charge. Logic took priority over romantic thoughts. She would finish reading his manuscript, return it to him and leave for Vienna.

Vienna? Why Vienna? She must go there. Someone's life depended on her being there.

Her thoughts alternated between calm rational analyzing and wild decisions without basis in logic. Forget Vienna. For the moment finish reading the book and return it to him.

Valerie's mother was surprised at the length of time her daughter remained in bed. She had always been an early riser.

It was 8 a.m. when, finally, she came down to the comfortable sitting room. As she entered she slipped the manuscript surreptitiously onto a coffee table, not wishing to speak of it. Her mother was an alert person and noticed the placing of the book, immediately asking if Valerie had had an opportunity to read sufficient to determine the standard of writing.

"Oh, the book. I just read a few paragraphs then fell asleep. Listen, mother, I think I must get away for a while. I want to be with you and talk but I also need to quietly re-establish myself. I would like to visit some exotic place for a week or so and revel in the joy of visions that were denied me for one year."

As the words poured forth, not only did she speak but she listened. She had not recognized herself, nor her actions or words, for the past forty-eight hours.

For a moment her mother was silent. She was obviously disappointed that Valerie would wish to be away from her at a time that seemed perfect for them to be together, added to which she wished to delight with her in the return of her sight. She realized that her disappointment was showing and quickly retorted that she understood completely. She was so happy that her daughter's eyes were once again not only beautiful. She would be there when Valerie returned, but could she just have some little insight into the relationship of Valerie with Roberto Grassina?

"Mother, there is no mystery. We met at the Blind Center and travelled on the train together. It was as simple as that." Simple it certainly was not, she thought to herself. "You know, I would just love a cup of tea." Her quick mind changed the subject. For the moment she wished to avoid any discussion concerning Roberto. It was an extraordinary sensation. She seemed to derive some erotic feeling just thinking of him but that was crazy. What happened on the train was terrible and frightening but now she found herself wanting the truth to be as he had said.

"Of course, dear, do you want Lapsang sushong?"

"No, that would be too strong. I think Earl Grey would be more relaxing."

They sat and sipped the tea together, casually chatting. Then the conversation arrived at the situation regarding Valerie's apartment. It was just around the corner; even so she had not been there for several weeks. This new matter succeeded in diverting them from the potential difficulty of more questions about Roberto.

"I feel better now. I think I will go around there and sort things out."

"OK, dear. Shall I prepare dinner for you or would you like to dine out?" As she spoke she realized that she was pressuring and quickly, before Valerie could reply, said, "Oh, no, I can't see you this evening. I've agreed to meet my friends at the bridge club. If you like I could ring and cancel it."

"No, that's fine, mother, you go to the bridge club and I will spend the evening at my apartment. I will call you tomorrow."

The doorman at the apartment block, seeing who was arriving in the taxi, instantly stepped forward to help Valerie, having no knowledge of the return of her sight.

Not wishing to get involved in long explanations, Valerie allowed him to take her arm. It was not difficult for her to feign blindness.

He opened the door, then handed her the key.

"Are you sure you'll be all right, miss?"

"I'm fine, thank you." She fumbled in her purse to find a couple of notes; however, before she could hand him the money he quickly left saying that he wanted nothing and was pleased to help.

"Just call me if you need me, miss."

"Thank you," she replied, then walked slowly in and closed the door.

She had had little confidence, during the preceding year, that she would ever see her home again. For a moment she just stood there, then closed and opened her eyes. It was true. She was awake. Then suddenly she had a feeling of fear. Someone was in the apartment. Instinctively she decided she should continue with her blind act.

She moved into the sitting room. There, on one of the armchairs, sat a middle-aged man in an old, dark tweed suit that bore the remains of many luncheons. On his head was a dirty, black beret and he wore thick glasses. His face was sad and had the look of someone who had suffered. She continued to move around the room with her arms outstretched and fingers fluttering, the feelers that she had relied on for a year to warn her of objects in her path and to recreate in her mind a picture of whatever they settled upon. She stopped and turned around.

"Is there someone there?"

He had wanted to speak and announce his presence but he was intrigued by the actions he witnessed, her delicate movements adding grace to her beauty.

"Forgive me. Did the porter not tell you that I am here? Please do not be alarmed."

"Who are you and what do you want with me?"

"My name is Miroslav Zdrazil. I have come to give you information concerning Baron Ernesto Grassina and his son Roberto."

"What makes you think that I would be interested?"

"Let me come straight to the point. My organization is holding Roberto Grassina."

"So you are terrorists."

"We do not consider ourselves terrorists. You may judge for yourself. We are holding Roberto as security on the outcome of a meeting that will determine the manner of division of a loan from the International Bank of Development and Reconstruction, a loan to be divided between the Czech and Slovak Republics. Baron Grassina heads the commission and is in a strong position to persuade the other delegates on the outcome of that division."

"That I would describe as terrorism."

"The outcome of the meeting is so vital to my group that your opinion is of no importance to us. If I may I will continue. What we wish you to do is to travel to Vienna, of your own free will. You will be met and taken to Roberto. The matter may then be quickly resolved."

Yet another strange coincidence. A short while ago something was telling her she must go to Vienna, that someone's life depended on her travelling there. Little did she imagine that once again Roberto Grassina would be that reason.

"I have no interest in Roberto Grassina. Now I intend to call the police."

"Please listen to what I have to say and then I will leave. We have threatened Roberto's life. He has no fear for himself but there are many others involved, including his father. We need someone to meet Baron Grassina and quietly tell him that we have his son. If you will undertake to perform this task, many lives will be saved including that of Roberto. Otherwise I can make no guarantees."

She hesitated for a moment. She wanted to be firm and throw him out, refusing absolutely to have any part of the matter. That would achieve nothing and Roberto must be very uncomfortable, having been moved so soon after his operation. She imagined him in some basement, tied and gagged. She must go to him. Not only that but the dream was now constantly in her mind. She felt that his father also needed her.

"Very well, I will go; however, if I have any indication that anyone is to suffer I will instantly inform the authorities of what I know. When must I leave?"

"Tomorrow morning at 10:15. Here is the ticket for the Lufthansa flight. I am sorry there is so little time. We had been waiting at the station to meet Roberto Grassina the day of the train crash, then with all that happened we lost forty-eight hours."

"I have no reason to believe anything you say, so I think it better that you leave now. I will catch the flight tomorrow and expect to see Roberto as soon as possible after my arrival."

The little man got up to leave, his head seeming to hang in shame. He believed her to be blind and consequently had no reason to put on an act. This was a man torn between right and wrong. His motive must be very strong or maybe he was under pressure from the organization.

He moved toward her, took her hand and gently kissed the back of it.

"Don't be afraid," he said. "I will protect you with my very life, if that is necessary. You are a very nice and good young woman. We will meet again in Vienna. May I remind you that the lives of Baron Grassina and his son would be in danger if you divulge anything I have told you."

"I must tell my mother. I will say that I intend to go to Vienna and then on to the music festival in Salzburg."

"That would be fine. I am sorry to tell you that I know your telephone is under surveillance. The organization is devoted to their cause and would kill Roberto instantly if they have any doubt that you will remain silent."

"Please let yourself out. I have very many things to attend to."

"Goodbye, I wish you a safe journey."

She wanted to also bid him farewell, but decided it important to exhibit strength and so remained silent.

Now that the door had closed behind him she could begin to act normally. She decided to ensure that he had left, though for some strange reason she had no doubt. In fact a quick check of the apartment showed that he had left.

Valerie went to the bedroom and began to pack a suitcase, then decided to have a look at the ticket. It was for the first-class cabin. Probably the organization would have someone on the aircraft to keep her under observation, a task made simpler in the more confined first-class section. The unfortunate element of that situation would be that she would be obliged to continue with her blind act.

Having prepared her luggage she decided to call her mother, who was surprised at the choice of Vienna as an 'exotic' destination. Valerie explained that she had wanted to visit the Salzburg festival for many years and had decided to combine that destination with her rest and recuperation.

Sleep evaded her. She heard every hour, half and quarter hour chime on the French carriage clock, a sound that normally imparted a feeling of peace and calm. This night it only served to remind her of the hours counting down to her meeting with Roberto. That was the all important event. She would be with him. They would talk and soon everything would be resolved.

Gradually the pleasant thought of being near to him lulled her and she drifted off to sleep and the dream. The same dream as the night before. This time there was a little more, still no sound until just before she awoke. The man she seemed to think of as the Baron stood to speak. A gunshot pierced the air with a sharp crack; he grasped his chest with both hands, then slumped across the table. There the dream ended. It was as though she had seen part two of a story unfolding before her.

Her eyes opened on the room that had been the last place she had seen one year ago. She glanced around at the quality furnishings, collected over the years, and the heavy drapes that had had no effect on the passage of light to her eyes on that terrible morning.

Now she was awakening to a new fright, but there was no time to be frightened, or even think. It was late. It had been 4 a.m. before she had been able to sleep at all, then a deep sleep and the dream that caused her to wake up late.

She telephoned the porter and asked him to call a taxi to take her to the airport. Then she completed her preparations, had a coffee and hurried downstairs to the foyer, where the taxi had just arrived.

THREE

In retrospect Valerie felt she had made the correct decision in continuing to conceal the return of her sight and in a further endeavor to mislead whoever was there to monitor her, she read a braille book throughout the flight, or rather went through the motions.

Whilst her fingers moved across the page, from her position toward the rear of the first class compartment, she was able to observe the other three passengers. At first she decided that the businessman, just to the left and forward of her seat, might not be a businessman at all. His appearance gave no suggestion that he might be an international terrorist either. Not that that was conclusive evidence. It seems that professional criminals invariably have the appearance of decent everyday people.

Gradually though, the other two passengers also became contenders. Right of her and forward was a young man, elegantly dressed, with an aloof aspect. On his knee was a lap top computer which he constantly operated with one finger that was so dexterous as to defy the eye.

He could be calculating the cost of heroin, designing an apartment block or fine tuning his position in the stock market. Valerie was unable to see the screen of his computer from her seat. Maybe he was analyzing the operation of the organization or entering further details of Valerie into an indestructible file.

Sitting furthest away from her was a very beautiful dark-haired girl, probably a model by her dress and rather exaggerated make-up. Every few moments she glanced around at Valerie, then half-way through the flight got up, walked back to where Valerie sat, and said, "Excuse me, I could not help noticing you. May I sit with you for a moment?"

"Certainly, it would be my pleasure."

"May I ask you? Have you always been blind?"

"No, I have been blind for one year."

"How did it happen?"

"I woke up one morning and found that I was unable to see."

"That is terrible and in that time you have learned to read braille, that's amazing. I have a brother who was born blind. Then about one year ago he suddenly gained his sight. It was a miracle."

The coincidence was too much. Obviously this was the sister of Roberto. Now she could even see a slight resemblance.

"My brother wrote a book while he was blind. It was a love story. In the book he described a girl from an image in his mind. When I saw you I was unable to take my eyes from you. It is just incredible, you seem to be exactly the girl he described. Because of his blindness he relied on touch to create a picture in his mind. He would touch my hair and say no, it's longer. Then he would feel the contours of my face and say that the cheek bones were not quite so pronounced. She is the same height, she has less make-up. He had heard of the different colours of hair and he felt that her hair was auburn, and that her eyes were soft, greenish-brown. As he built up a description of the beautiful girl I began to see her, probably as he did. He telephoned me yesterday. I didn't even know he was in Vienna. He was very anxious that I join him there. Please allow me to introduce myself. My name is Claudia Grassina. My brother's name is Roberto."

"I am pleased to meet you, my name is Valerie." She held out her hand, being careful to be inaccurate, emphasizing once more her 'blindness.'

"Are you going to Vienna on holiday?" Claudia asked.

"Yes, I want to tour the city, then take a few days to visit the Salzburg music festival. I have always wanted to go there." She managed to suppress the desire to speak about Roberto. His sister being there on the plane, she thought, could be dangerous. Or maybe it was part of the process. Soon she would discover the answer.

Claudia insisted on taking Valerie's arm and assisting her through passport and customs control. After completion of the formalities they were met by the little man with the black beret.

"I see you have met," he said.

Simultaneously the girls asked, "Who are you?" "Who is there?"

Addressing Claudia he said,

"My name is Miroslav Zdrazil. Roberto asked me to meet you here." Then turning to Valerie, "We met yesterday. I have a car waiting, please come with me. Soon you will meet Roberto."

Claudia in astonishment turned to Valerie. "So you know Roberto. Why did you say nothing during the flight?"

"Forgive me. The whole thing is very complicated. I think you will shortly know what is going on."

"What is going on? I refuse to go anywhere with anyone, until I know what has happened to my brother."

"Please control yourself," Zdrazil cautioned. "I can only tell you that Roberto's life depends on your action. He has been injured and needs your help. Valerie is also here to help Roberto. Please hurry, we need to go to him quickly."

Claudia coloured with anger, but she obviously loved her brother dearly because she joined the other two and went to the car without another word.

"How were you able to meet us?" Valerie asked Zdrazil, "I took an overnight flight."

As they walked toward the car, Valerie glanced at the licence plate and noticed that it had a different letter and number configuration from the majority of cars that came and went around the airport. It also had an additional plate which bore the letters SK. She had a good knowledge of the international country identification letters, but this one puzzled her. Maybe an African state, she thought.

"We have about a two-hour journey, then you will be able to speak to Roberto and everything will be clear to you both."

The Mercedes left the airport and headed east, Valerie judged by the sun's position. Signs appeared indicating Bratislava and Budapest. Bratislava, that is the capital of the newly formed Slovak Republic, she thought to herself. So that's what SK indicated. Obviously their destination would be in Slovakia.

Sure enough, after passing a few small Austrian villages, they arrived at the border of Austria and the Republic of Slovakia. Valerie was amazed at the informality of crossing the frontier. There seemed to be little interest in cars, though there were long lines of articulated lorries from Russia, Bulgaria, Greece and many other eastern countries standing idle. Presumably the drivers were being confronted with exaggerated bureaucracy

Shortly after, they were crossing the Danube to the historic city of Bratislava, which presented little hindrance to their passage. Valerie began to feel satisfied with herself. She had managed to deceive them into thinking she was blind and yet she was able to take an interest in her surroundings. She had never been to any Eastern European countries before and felt a certain excitement. There was a discernible air of mystery.

She was, of course, apprehensive and a little frightened but did not really believe she was in danger. Her main concern was for Roberto.

The journey continued and twenty minutes after leaving the city the car turned onto an unpaved road for half a mile or so and then arrived at a farm entrance. As they approached the farm buildings, Valerie began to see that they were deserted. Old rusty farm implements stood in front of broken sheds and where once there had been agricultural activity now there was tall grass and weeds.

The car came to a stop in front of the old farmhouse. On the steps sat two young men with Kalishnikov rifles across their laps.

Zdrazil turned to the girls and said, "Please do not be alarmed. We have no intention of harming either of you, though I must insist that you remain quiet and do as you are told. It is the life of Roberto that is at stake."

The two young men stood and stepped aside as Zdrazil led the way down the hall and into a dimly lit room. There, on a bed, lay Roberto. He didn't look at all well; his face was white and he bore many bruises and cuts, in addition to which the plaster cast on his leg was dappled red with blood.

"You bastards," Claudia snapped. "What have you done to him?" Zdrazil ignored the outburst and left the room.

The girls moved to either side of the bed on which Roberto lay and took his hands.

"Don't worry. I'm OK," Roberto assured them. "I'm sorry to involve you in this terrible matter. I had no choice, they knew everything about you and threatened to kill you both if I did not cooperate."

"What do they want? And who are they?" Claudia asked, her voice trembling with fear and anger.

"From what I can gather, Zdrazil is almost certainly the leader of the group. As you know, on the 1st of January of this year, the republic of Czechoslovakia was divided into two new countries: the Slovak Republic, which historically had closer ties to Hungary, and the Czech Republic, which, despite the atrocities of the second world war, had its traditions and cultures more closely linked to Austria and Germany. Slovakia felt that the Prague government maintained a two-tier division of the country's wealth that discriminated against the southern state, which sustains uneconomic heavy industry and inefficient farming. The Slovak people constantly agitated for separation and the Czech Republic raised no objection to granting Slovakia its independence. At the time of the collapse of Eastern Europe a special Bank was established to channel funds to worthy applicants."

"So that's the connection. Father is currently involved in negotiations with the Czech and Slovak Republics on the division of funds to those two countries." Claudia began to realize their involvement. "They have kidnapped you to hold you hostage against father's decision."

"That's right."

"Now I can see why they took you, but where do Valerie and I fit in?"

"They know that you are a trained nurse. You are here to administer what medical help you can to me. Valerie will be the messenger and will be taken to meet father this evening. Because of her blindness," he intelligently made no comment on the fact that she was, once more, behaving as a sightless person, "they believe that she will be allowed to come close to father. She will tell him that you and I have been taken by a group who intend to kill us both if the bulk of the international loan does not go to Slovakia. At the moment no one else knows of my kidnapping or that you two have also been brought here under duress. Obviously if the committee learned of the action of this group, to pressurize and influence the channelling of funds, they would immediately suspend father from his position as chairman."

"But surely, even if the funds do go to Slovakia, they will have to kill us, because once we are released we would expose the Slovak government."

"These people are not of the Slovak government, although they appear to be in a position whereby they can access the funds. Once they have their hands on the money, they will release us, so they say."

Whilst awaiting their arrival Roberto, with his knowledge of braille, had embossed a note for Valerie on a small piece of paper, utilizing the cap of a pen. He passed the note to Valerie and noticed that she took it without having to be guided to it. Claudia noticed the passing of the note but did not realize that to take it, as she did, Valerie had to be able to see.

Valerie ran her fingers over the note which read, 'THIS ROOM IS BUGGED.'

Her fingers had just deciphered the last word when Zdrazil burst into the room and snapped, "Give me that piece of paper." Obviously Roberto was correct in his belief that nothing was going unseen.

Valerie held up the note and Zdrazil took it.

"What does it say? There is nothing here." As she read the note Valerie had squeezed the paper between her fingers, thus flattening the cryptic indentations. Roberto quickly retorted that he had noticed tears in Valerie's eyes and gave her the paper to dry away the tears.

Zdrazil was evidently satisfied with the explanation and went on to say, "All three of you are now aware of the situation. As I have told you we have no wish to harm anyone." Then turning to Claudia, "You may attend to your brother's injuries and this evening I will take Valerie to meet your father." He took Valerie's arm and said, "Come with me."

Valerie was so relieved that her small mistake had apparently gone unnoticed that she obeyed and followed Zdrazil without question. He led her to the adjoining room.

In the room was a table, a chair and a suitcase full of clothing. On one wall, suspended on a nail, a beautiful, black, sequin-covered gown hung limply. It looked most out of place where a solitary light bulb lit the room and dust, cracked walls and bare floor boards contrasted with the luxury and glamour of the dress.

Zdrazil led her across to where the dress hung and lifted her hand to touch the material.

"You must prepare yourself well. Tonight you will be present at an important function. When you are ready, give me a call and I will come and guide you back to join your friends."

It was doubtful that the room was also under surveillance, even so Valerie could take no chances. She dressed laboriously, emphasizing all her actions to convince any potential onlooker that she was in fact blind.

Once ready she called Zdrazil who led her back to join Claudia and Roberto. Both were taken aback at how beautiful she looked and they recalled a passage in Roberto's book where the heroine also entered a room dressed in such a gown. It was truly amazing how the fiction of the novel again manifested itself in reality.

They both remarked on her appearance and as Valerie joined them, Claudia handed her the black high-heeled shoes she had been wearing. The masters of the great plan had omitted to bring shoes to be worn with the black dress and the brown low heels that formed part of Valerie's travelling wardrobe looked quite ridiculous. Valerie made no move to take the shoes and Claudia touched her arm saying, "Here, take my shoes to complete your wardrobe. My shoes are black, as is the dress. Would you like me to assist you with your make-up?"

"Thank you, that would be very kind of you." For a few moments Claudia left her brother and employed her other skill, in perfecting the finishing touches to Valerie's make-up. Once that was completed she returned to her brother's side and continued to clean his wounds and apply fresh bandages and band-aids.

Roberto felt a sense of pride in the vision of Valerie, but why? The last time they had spoken she was contemplating how she would go about denouncing him and his actions on the runaway train.

Valerie noticed how his eyes travelled slowly over her whole body, revelling in her beauty. She could see the pleasure he derived from what he saw and was pleased that he saw her so. Even so the memory of that terrible encounter on the train flashed back vividly to her. How could she continue with this charade? Once more that alternating sensation, a conflict of anger and aggression toward him, and the strange desire to be close to him. She felt that she never wanted to leave his side again.

The feelings had to remain within her head, considering it important that their captors believed her to be blind. She drank a little coffee but felt unable to eat anything. Zdrazil remarked that she may be pleased she had declined the thick, dry sandwiches when soon she would have her choice of exquisite delicacies.

Zdrazil and Valerie were taken in the Mercedes back to Bratislava, from where they continued up to the castle overlooking the Danube. She had noticed a sticker on the windshield. Although it had no meaning to her, being in Slovak language, it was evidently the pass for entry to the castle, because once the gate patrol had scrutinized it, they were permitted passage.

Valerie had always enjoyed a passion for architectural history and revelled in the magnificence of the castle structure. They moved, with the other arriving guests, into the dining room, where over the head table hung a placard, bearing the words 'Slovak Peoples Democratic Union.' For the moment the seats at the head table were empty but she felt sure she would soon see Roberto's father sitting there.

Her dream was beginning to become reality and her heart began to beat fast in anticipation of what might happen.

Zdrazil continued to guide her, then apparently caught sight of someone he knew. Suddenly he changed direction and led Valerie to a group standing by a window where they looked out over the Danube, with the twinkling lights of Austria on the horizon. It was a clear moonlit night and the view was magnificent.

"Ambassador Novak, I would like to introduce you to Roberto's fiance. Roberto was unable to attend and wished to have his father meet Valerie. It will be a great surprise to him because Roberto only met her recently, and they fell in love instantly." Valerie began to fume at this ridiculous nonsense but once more suppressed her desire to tell all.

"I can understand why Roberto would be attracted to such a charming and beautiful young woman. He is a very lucky young man," Novak said as he took Valerie's hand.

"You are very kind. I am pleased to meet you and look forward to meeting the Baron."

"We have about fifteen minutes before the function begins. Come with me and I will introduce you immediately. No doubt the Baron will be fired with new enthusiasm when he meets you. Please follow me."

Novak led them out through the main entrance of the dining hall and down a short passage to a room where two men, probably security guards, stood by the door. They nodded acknowledgment to Novak and opened the door as Novak led Valerie and Zdrazil into the room.

It was a very large reception room with massive paintings and groups of weapons mounted on the walls: muskets, crossbows, armor and lances, draped with flags from the period of the Austro-Hungarian Empire. Above the massive hearth one bright new flag proudly hung, the flag of the newly formed Republic of Slovakia.

In a robust leather chair facing the fire-place sat the distinguished figure of the Baron, one hand above his head holding the back of the chair and exhibiting a thick ring, the other resting casually on the arm of the chair; between his fingers a dark cigar that filled the air of the room with an aroma that spelt Cuba.

Hearing the entry of the group he turned his head and caught sight of Valerie. Instantly his eyes lit up and he stood to greet her, paying little attention to the other two.

Novak stepped forward. "Sir, I have the great pleasure to introduce you to your son's fiance, Valerie." Then turning to her, "This is Baron Ernesto Grassina."

Valerie held out her trembling hand, which the Baron took as he bowed slightly forward and gently kissed the back of it. He noticed her white stick and insecure movements and conjectured, "I imagine that the fact you are blind has something to do with how you met my son."

"Indeed. That is quite correct. We met at the Blind Institute in the Black Forest."

"But tell me how long have you known each other. He didn't mention you even as recently as two weeks ago when we last spoke on the telephone."

"We met just a few days ago. Ambassador Novak and Mr. Zdrazil are both premature in referring to me as your son's fiance. We are simply friends."

"Whatever, I am very pleased to make your acquaintance and would be happy to speak to you later, if you will grant me that pleasure. After the dinner I have to give a speech, following which I will be free. Perhaps you would care to join me for drinks in my hotel room, so that I might get to know you a little better. But tell me, where is Roberto?" The question came out of the blue and Valerie had no prepared answer. Before she could even begin to try to think up some story, Zdrazil interjected, "Unfortunately Roberto has had a slight automobile accident. It is not serious but his leg was broken and it will be in a cast for the next six weeks. He is in Vienna and will call you tomorrow."

"This is too much. Why was I not informed? Very well, I must join the other guests now. Valerie, please accept my invitation, if only to give me news of my son. Will you?"

"I will be pleased to tell you all I know."

"Thank you. Then we will meet again later." He kissed her hand once more, then left the room.

Zdrazil turned to Novak and asked to be excused to speak to Valerie for a moment. Novak smiled, turned and followed the Baron.

"Valerie, I must warn you that if we have the slightest indication that you give any information other than that which we have discussed, both Roberto and Claudia will be killed. There is no way you can find the farm and if you even try the guards have been instructed to kill them and leave. I suggest that you follow my instructions, then in time you will all be freed and we will be gone. We have planned for months and will stop at nothing to complete the operation successfully."

"I will do as you say."

"Very well. So we are clear. As you told the Baron, you met Roberto at the Blind Institute. You will say that you were instantly attracted to one another and have been in each other's company ever since. Then you will tell him that a group, you don't know who, is holding Roberto and Claudia and that they intend to kill them if he does not convince the committee to channel the bulk of the fund to the Slovak Republic."

"I understand."

"That is very intelligent of you. Now let's return to the dining hall and enjoy the evening."

FOUR

Valerie was seated at a table with Zdrazil, Novak and several other officials. They were speaking Slovak, a language that seemed to her to be similar to Russian, though she had no knowledge or understanding of either language and consequently paid little attention, leaving her free to enjoy the atmosphere. Being 'blind' she was obliged to control her head and eye movements. Even so she was still able to take great pleasure in the architecture, heavy antique furniture, crystal chandeliers and wine glasses and the elegance of the other guests present.

The meal was excellent and after a long day with little opportunity to eat, Valerie revelled in the new culinary delights, occasionally losing sight of the reason she was there. The grandeur and opulence of the occasion satisfied her interest in those matters and following her most recent experiences was a welcome contrasting situation.

Zdrazil could be quite charming paying her, as he did, a great deal of attention. Apparently he sincerely wished her to be comfortable and enjoy herself. Once all the guests had been served with the main course she leaned across to where he sat and whispered, ensuring that Novak did not hear, not knowing his involvement or otherwise in the matter.

"I am obliged to say that I am surprised at the contrast in your behavior and your involvement in kidnapping and embezzlement."

"My dear Valerie, each of us has a price. I have served my country for the past thirty years and have nothing to show for my loyalty. Tell me how much would buy you?" He did not wait for her reply. "Just imagine that you were offered three million dollars to continue your relationship with Roberto, be absolutely safe from discovery and live a life of luxury. Can you honestly tell me that you would reject the offer?"

"We are not speaking only of money. We are speaking of kidnapping and threatening someone's life. You appear to know the Baron. How close have you been to the family?"

"I have known Roberto since he was born. I love him like a son. You must understand that I have no future. I saw my parents lose everything they had worked all their lives for. While I was a boy my mother returned home late each evening, her hands bleeding from scrubbing with wire wool the stone products made in my father's factory. They lost the business and their savings, simply annulled by the communist authorities. I am too old to have any possibility of success. I feel that I almost owe it to my parents to take back all they lost and much more. I am to receive a considerable sum, you cannot imagine how much. The plan has been devised with the intent to carry out any action necessary to ensure success, though we are confident that there will be no need to kill anyone."

"If you have suffered and seen others suffer why would you now inflict suffering?"

"I think that you're exaggerating. I was very sorry that Roberto received injuries during his questioning. Had I known that it would be so I would not have become involved. That is over. There will be no more pain for anyone and things have gone too far to turn back. You can help to make things go smoothly, with the consequent reduction in the risk of anyone's being hurt. In ten days the money will be divided amongst us and we will be gone. If you do as I told you there is no reason for anyone to suffer."

Before Valerie could reply there was a call for silence. Baron Ernesto Grassina was about to give his speech. She turned in the direction of the head table. There before her was the scene, exactly as she had witnessed it in her dream. Her first reaction was to jump to her feet and try to stop the proceedings. But who would believe her? And if they did believe she had had a dream it would surely be insufficient reason to justify changing anything.

The room fell silent. The Baron rose to his feet, glanced around the dining hall and filled his lungs but before he could even begin to speak a shot rang out. Valerie's dream continued to replay as she saw him grasp at his chest with both hands then slump across the table.

The previous silence was suddenly replaced with screams and confusion. Fortunately the quick actions of security guards resulted in the assassin being apprehended immediately.

Valerie trembled with horror and shame. He had been shot. Maybe she could have prevented it if she had spoken out. She should have acted. How could she ever forgive herself, believing there was a potential danger and not taking some action. It had been an unrealistic situation. Like everyone else she had had dreams in her life that reflected places and events. Dreams that occasionally seemed to predict to a minor extent, though previously there had been nothing of any consequence. She began to feel different in some strange way. Something was happening to her and she didn't understand.

The guests had been very anxious to hear the Baron's speech and had failed to notice that toward the rear of the dining hall a man had a pistol aimed in the direction of the Baron. At first his aim was for the head. Then just as he began to increase his pressure on the trigger he moved the gun to a new alignment. The heart would be his target. Why had he changed? He did not know, he always shot his victims through the head.

When Valerie pictured the repeated scene from her dream she had prayed, with a concentration she had never before capable of, that nothing would happen to the Baron. She could not know that it was her intense will that had had the power to change the aim of the gunman.

Zdrazil took Valerie's arm and invited her to go with him.

They hurried through the throng of frightened people, though their progress was hindered by the desire of all the guests to leave the dining hall or to go to Baron Grassina, anxious to discover his condition and pray that his injuries may not be so serious as at first they appeared.

Finally they arrived at the reception room where they had met the Baron before going to dinner. Cushions had been placed on the floor in front of the fire and the Baron was lying on them. He had been covered with two or three top-coats. Novak was already there, white and visibly shaken. He nervously shouted at one of the others nearby. Valerie recognized the word ambulance. Before the man could reply the doors burst open and two white-coated men with a stretcher entered the room, with them a doctor, by his bag and stethoscope. They hurried to where the Baron lay, the coats were lifted carefully away and the doctor began his examination.

The room was quiet, though it was still possible to hear the continued confusion next door in the great hall and in the corridor outside.

After a few moments the doctor sat back on his ankles, smiled, spoke a few words to Novak, then turned to the white-coated men, apparently instructing them to attend to the Baron. They stepped forward and lifted him carefully on to the stretcher, then carried him from the room. As they did so Novak seemed to breathe a sigh of relief. He made a statement to those who remained in the room, then got up and followed the ambulance crew.

Zdrazil calmly relayed Novak's message to Valerie. The Baron was not seriously injured. He was being taken to the hospital for a complete examination and would be back in his hotel later.

Valerie could not comment that she had seen him fall across the table. That would expose her ability to see, though if she had, Zdrazil would have satisfied her surprise when he said that fortunately the Baron had been wearing a bullet-proof vest, as he was obliged to do always when in a public place. The vest had stopped the bullet but the impact had winded him. Otherwise he appeared to be unharmed.

Valerie was relieved and overjoyed that the Baron was not seriously hurt though she was puzzled that the premonition of her dream, such an extraordinary and powerful event, should end thus, like a damp squib.

That fear having been overcome, Valerie and Zdrazil, together, began to say, "But who shot him, and why?"

"Come with me," Zdrazil instructed. "We will answer those two questions."

Zdrazil obviously knew the castle well and also where the assailant would be taken. He led Valerie down a cold, dimly lit, spiral stone staircase to a room where there was a great deal of activity, with people coming and going.

Valerie was unable to distinguish between the police and soldiers who wore very similar uniforms. Whichever they were, they were in abundance.

Zdrazil led her to one side of the room where there was a leather chair and invited her to sit while he made enquiries. She did as suggested and watched as he passed, yet again unhindered, through massive wooden doors. Zdrazil was evidently a very important and respected person.

While the door was open, for the moment of his entry to the room, she heard moaning. Someone, probably the gunman, was obviously in great distress. Then once again the door was closed.

In the anteroom, where she sat, there were perhaps thirty people, distinguished ladies and gentlemen in evening dress. Some of the young women wore colorful national costumes and everyone spoke in subdued tones apparently straining their ears to hear what transpired in the inner room. Valerie also concentrated her attention in that direction, although all she could hear was intermittent shouting, words that had no meaning for her.

Suddenly there was a terrifying scream, that caused Valerie to shudder. Then silence. After a few moments Zdrazil came from the room looking very glum. Valerie almost forgot her act and was about to comment on his disconsolate appearance, fortunately he spoke first, "The assassin is dead, but worse, he died before divulging anything."

"How did he die? Were the interrogators too violent?"

"It is a mystery. I have seen such an expression before, just once. The condition is referred to in medical terms as 'Catavaric Spasm.' All the joints stiffen and the eyes bulge in a state of absolute terror. It is a puzzle; however, the important thing is that the Baron is virtually unharmed. I think that we may now go to him."

Zdrazil took Valerie's arm and began to lead her out of the room, as he did so he whispered, "I believe that you and I are quite clear on what you will say to the Baron. Now I will take you to the Hotel where a room has been reserved for you. Everything you need will be there. Then I must go to the farm. We will meet again tomorrow."

While he spoke he guided her out of the castle and back to the Mercedes. The driver seemed very relieved to see Zdrazil and nervously relayed a message to him, in response to which Zdrazil made a call on the car-phone. The conversation was brief but evidently very significant because Zdrazil became very agitated. This time, though, he told Valerie nothing, suggesting that he may be thinking he had said too much already.

The Mercedes moved quietly and quickly to the hotel by the Danube where the Baron was lodged. Not a word was spoken for the five minutes or so of the journey, which gave Valerie the opportunity to ponder the extraordinary chain of events to which she had been witness.

Once again, at the hotel, Zdrazil seemed to be able to command anything that was necessary. At the reception desk, where he was apparently well-known, a key for a suite was given to him, which he handed to Valerie, then a note from the Baron which stated that he was feeling well and still would be happy to see Valerie, if she felt up to it. Valerie confirmed that she had no problem and would go to his room in thirty minutes.

Zdrazil took his leave of her and said that he would collect her in the morning at 10 a.m. Then he left.

Valerie's suite was palatial, certainly intended for foreign guests only. There were three rooms and two bathrooms. The bed was very inviting, firm and luxurious, though for the moment Valerie was more interested in her forthcoming meeting with the Baron.

She went through to the dressing room, where she found a closet full of elegant clothes and shoes, unlike the situation at the farm, with the gown hanging on a nail. She decided to change. The black dress was beautiful though now she felt the desire for something light and pastel, thinking that it may relieve the tension of the forthcoming meeting.

She chose a pale yellow, slim fitting cocktail dress with a length that exhibited her very shapely legs. Not that she wished to provoke the Baron, but he was the father of Roberto and she was anxious that he should also find her attractive. He had been attentive on their first encounter which she felt had been a sincere pleasure in her appearance for his son's sake.

Unlike the oversight at the farm, she found there were shoes to match each dress. Valerie was intrigued that even the size was correct. Everything had been planned very thoroughly.

Having dressed and prepared herself to her complete satisfaction, she called the Baron's room number. Shortly after his butler knocked gently on the door of her suite. He took her arm and led her along the hall past a couple of other suites to that of the Baron.

"Come in, my dear," the Baron invited. May I offer you a drink?"

"Yes, I would like a dry sherry."

"Certainly." He turned to the butler and repeated Valerie's request.

She enquired how he felt after his ordeal and was reassured that he had suffered no physical harm. He was shaken and sad, feeling as he did that the attempt on his life was almost certainly as a result of his pioneering a bill in the European parliament, aimed at reducing subsidies to farmers. He had received many threats, but as he pointed out, even if his adversaries were successful in killing him the work would continue in the hands of someone else.

After receiving their drinks they made themselves comfortable on Louis XIV chairs and the Baron released his butler for the evening.

"Tell me, Valerie, I am very anxious to know how Roberto is and how he came to be involved in a car accident."

Valerie placed her drink on the onyx table and replied, "You may have noticed that I had no difficulty in finding the table for my glass. The fact is that I am no longer blind. I continue with the act because I find myself in a very dangerous and difficult situation. My feeling is that if I am believed to be blind, it could, and has been beneficial. The situation involves not only Roberto but also Claudia." At this point the Baron began to interrupt. Valerie calmed him and asked that he permit her to explain everything, after which he could ask her questions.

"Fine. Please continue. I agree that that would be the best policy."

"My association with Roberto began on a runaway train. We were both passengers when it crashed during the descent of a mountain in the Black Forest. Apparently you were not informed. Prior to the impact I was blind, having lost my sight one year previously. The impact caused me to receive a severe blow to the head which stunned me for a moment but when I recovered I found that I had regained my sight completely. In the accident Roberto lost a considerable amount of blood from an injury to his leg." She purposely avoided making reference to what had transpired between Roberto and herself prior to the impact. "We were both taken to hospital where it was discovered that I had the same very unusual blood group as that of Roberto. A fortunate coincidence because the surgeon, who was to operate, had been unsuccessful in finding a donor." She continued, "That incident has since been overshadowed. You must prepare yourself for a shock. The fact is that Zdrazil is involved with a group that is intending to steal funds from the World Bank of Development and Reconstruction." At this point the Baron could contain himself no longer and tried once more to interrupt. Valerie, however, pointed out that she thought it necessary for him to know all the facts before he spoke or took action that might further compound the situation. He agreed and asked her to continue.

"Roberto and Claudia are currently being held at an old farm some 40 km from Bratislava. I was also taken there, against my will, but released to come here and relay the group's demand, which is that you ensure that the committee channel the bulk of the proposed fund to the Slovak Republic. The group has some means of accessing the money. They say that once they have removed what they want they will release Claudia and Roberto. Thereafter they will disappear without a trace and so will many millions of dollars." The Baron listened intently as Valerie went on to say, "Zdrazil took little precaution when taking me to the farm or bringing me here, believing me to be blind. It was clear to me that the driver took unnecessary diversions in an attempt to confuse me. Even so, I am confident that I can give you a map that will allow the farm to be located. I must return there tomorrow morning with Zdrazil. He will call for me at 10 a.m. It is best that I return so as to give them confidence that all is proceeding as planned. You are obviously shocked to discover that Zdrazil is a member of the group. He told me how close he has been to your family. The problem is that if someone so trusted can prove unreliable then it could be dangerous to speak of the matter to anyone."

"You are evidently a very resourceful and intelligent young lady," the Baron said, full of admiration. "A rare find in one so beautiful. I would be most concerned at the thought of your returning to the farm. Tell me, how seriously injured is Roberto?"

"He has a deep wound on the inside of his thigh. His leg is in a cast and the surgeon advised me that he would have to remain that way for at least six weeks, following which he will need a program of rehabilitation. The group took his sister to administer to him in her capacity as a nurse."

"I shall refrain from self-pity or concentrating on the obvious ifs and whys," the Baron said in a somber mood. "The important thing is that you should not be subjected to any further danger. Furthermore, somehow my son and daughter must be rescued from the farm. You are quite right that it is almost impossible to be one hundred percent sure of allegiance from anyone; however, there is one man I have had with me for the past twenty years. He has proven himself many times and I am quite sure that he would never betray me. May I ask you to remain with me for a further twenty minutes, during which time I will call Karl to join us, he is my right hand man. You can then explain to him the whereabouts of the farm and we may also try to obtain some device that you can wear, giving us the possibility of locating you at any time."

"Of course. I will do anything I can to help."

The Baron made a call and was about to speak once more when Valerie asked, "Now, may I ask you one or two things that I think it is important for me to know?"

"Certainly, my dear, please go ahead."

"Is it really possible that you can persuade the committee to decide to channel the funds to the Slovak Republic?"

"Probably. The rest of the committee are my colleagues of many years' standing and invariably follow my recommendations."

"Once the decision has been reached, how much time would elapse before the funds are transferred to the respective authorities in Bratislava?"

"The World Bank of Development and Reconstruction has been in operation for approximately five years and has at its disposal a substantial sum. Because during its period of existence funds have not been allocated in relation to what has been available, there is, in fact, a huge surplus in the vaults. The amount involved that would be made available to the Slovak Republic, if that were to be the recipient country, could be of the order of $300,000,000. A sum sufficient to tempt the loyalty of anyone who had the possibility to access it, though I am still shocked that Miroslav has been persuaded. As to the transfer, once agreement has been reached, it would be almost immediate."

During the course of their anticipation of the arrival of Karl they spoke with great enthusiasm of their new-found friendship and of Valerie's relationship to Roberto and Claudia.

The twenty minutes passed very rapidly and pleasantly. Soon the discussion became concentrated on concrete action. Karl had brought with him a miniature transmitter and gave instructions to Valerie on how to conceal it. Then, while she went to the bathroom to follow the instructions, the Baron explained the situation to Karl.

Once the transmitter was sufficiently well hidden, Valerie called to Karl to switch on the receiver, following which they completed a test. This was followed by Valerie drawing a map of the location of the farm. She cautioned that there were armed guards. She had seen only two, though there might be others.

All arrangements were completed and it was agreed that Valerie would return to the farm in the morning with Zdrazil. Nothing would be attempted for three days, giving the group confidence that Valerie had followed Zdrazil's instructions and given no other information. At 4 a.m. on Tuesday morning, Valerie would switch on the battery power to the transmitter, giving her location. By that time a rescue team would have been assembled and would quickly and efficiently disarm and apprehend Zdrazil's group.

Following all the preparations Valerie bade good night to the Baron and was accompanied to her suite by Karl. In the short period Valerie had been in the company of Karl she found him to be a man who inspired trust. They confirmed their appointment for Tuesday and parted at her door.

Valerie kicked off her shoes as she closed the door behind herself. The desire to slip into the warm, bubbling spa was similar to being extremely hungry. She almost could not wait.

From the door to the spa a trail of clothing scattered in all directions. Then the warmth as her body became suspended in the water, which enveloped her with a sense of luxury and comfort.

Slowly all the tension melted away. She was able, for the first time in many days, to sample absolute relaxation.

A thin vapor mist hung over the marble tub and she drank in the pleasure. For fifteen minutes or so her mind drifted in emptiness, peaceful and calm. Then slowly the matter of her circumstances filtered back into her thoughts.

She began to analyze all the events, many of which seemed beyond explanation; her extraordinary instinct to protect Roberto, the dream of the shooting of the Baron that manifested itself in reality and her decision to continue with the act of blindness, the condition that had initiated the whole nightmare but that had already proven fruitful.

There had to be some ethereal reason why she had lost her sight and Roberto had gained his. Then the massive train crash that permitted only two survivors. It appeared there was something beyond the realm of normality manipulating events.

Her eyes had remained closed during her immersion in the water, then, as she became perfectly relaxed, she began to open them. She watched the movement of the mist above the water and saw the condensation on the gold coloured faucets. A drip of water ran down the cold tap, collecting small water droplets in it's path. Valerie half closed her eyes and studied the shape that had formed on the shiny surface. It's a tree, she thought. Not simply a tree, a dead tree with bare branches stretching upward. She was too tired to pay any further attention. What did it matter anyway. She certainly had no interest in a dead tree. The important matter, at that particular moment, was to get to bed and so she did.

FIVE

Olin and Jiri had hunted pheasant in the area for many years. Dusk had fallen, with a good bag, and they were anxious to get to the old farmhouse, as they always did after a hunt. There they would drink beer, eat bread and hard salami and reminisce on how things used to be better.

Their presence did not go unnoticed by the guards, who stepped back inside the entrance to the farmhouse. One hurried to where Claudia and Roberto spoke happily together. Strange that this terrible situation should bring them together after such a long time. She had been busy with her career, he with the completion of his book. They did telephone once a month and every Christmas the whole family converged on Florence, to the family house. There Roberto and Claudia joined the rest of the family in great festivities, an occasion of particular importance because of the guaranteed presence of their father.

It is sad, they agreed, that a family that had been so close should drift apart. Modern day living dictated that it should be so, each following their own interests and careers. Their compelled proximity, in the current situation, highlighted the ever increasing frequency of being separated and they vowed that, once they were free of their captors, they would find time for each other and their father, whatever and however important the projects in which they were involved.

"Shut up," snapped the guard in subdued terms, pointing his weapon in their direction. He had used his entire English vocabulary in one phrase, but it was sufficient. The siblings did as instructed, which caused the guard to feel very satisfied with himself that he had learned such a useful English expression, one that had proven so effective.

At the entrance the second guard crouched low and retained one of the hunters in his sights. He prayed that they would change direction. Zdrazil would not be happy, but what could he do if they continued toward the farmhouse?

The hunters didn't change direction and as they entered the farmhouse the guard made his presence known, ordering them to throw their weapons to the floor.

Jiri and Olin were so shocked by this unexpected event that they did as instructed without hesitation. They stood shaking and wide-eyed, in disbelief at the circumstance in which they found themselves.

"Do as you are told and no harm will come to you. Step into the first room on the left and keep your hands above your heads. Move slowly and do not speak." At this point the other guard joined them from the room where Claudia and Roberto were held, having first locked the door behind himself.

The two hunters continued into the room until they reached the opposite wall. There they stood, with no confidence that their captors were sincere in that they had no intention of harming them, and waited.

One of the guards handed his rifle to his colleague then poked Jiri with his finger telling him to place his hands behind his back. He then tied him securely. Subsequently he diverted his attention to Olin and went through the same procedure. Having done so he then gyrated the hunters so that they were back to back and secured them together. The end of the rope he tossed over a ceiling beam and made a slipknot around the necks of his prisoners, a foolproof system.

"Just keep quiet and still. That way you will have no problems," he ordered. Then he joined the other guard and they left the room.

"I will call Zdrazil's driver and tell him what has happened," one of the guards muttered. The other agreed.

He made the call, leaving a message with the driver for when Zdrazil left the function at the castle. They anticipated that Zdrazil would order them to leave the farm immediately. Obviously it would not be too long before the hunters would be missed. People would begin looking. They would have to be gone before that time. It was agreed that one would remain to guard the prisoners whilst the other went to collect the ambulance once more.

He began the journey without his weapon, first walking to the main road, then by good fortune succeeding in thumbing a lift to Bratislava. There remained only a couple of kilometers to walk on arrival at the city center. There Zdrazil had a contact with a converted old Citröen, the vehicle that had served as the ambulance, when it was utilized to transport Roberto to the farm two days previously. Payment had been effected quickly and generously on the first occasion, consequently there was no problem in availability of the vehicle. Soon he was on his way back to the farm. Zdrazil will be pleased that I used my initiative, he thought.

Back at the farm once more it was just an hour before the call came from Zdrazil. He instructed them to transfer Claudia and Roberto, as the guards had anticipated, to his own house west of the city. Zdrazil would join them there approximately two hours later. He would call the house and tell his wife to expect them.

There was no stretcher available, consequently Roberto had to be helped to the 'Ambulance.' A painful operation, not only for him but also for Claudia having to see him suffer. Every bump of the unpaved road jolted the leg and gave considerable pain, though Roberto exercised great restraint in suppressing any reaction, not wishing to upset Claudia further.

Once on the main road the soft suspension of the Citröen was capable of levelling any small irregularities in the surface of the road and Roberto was more comfortable for the half-hour journey.

The wrought iron gates of Zdrazil's house were already open on their arrival and the Citröen drove straight in and parked behind the house. From there, once more, the painful transfer to the bed, already prepared on the third floor.

The stairs proved the most difficult. It was not only the pain, also the feeling of helplessness concerned Roberto. Here he was, involved in a situation that demanded courage and strength. Without strength and agility all the planning imaginable was useless; nevertheless, the eyes that had been still for so many years were very active, constantly looking for any possible weakness in their captors' control of them.

He longed for the return of Valerie, though he also was concerned for her safety and would have preferred that she escape from the situation. It would be better if she did not believe him. It would be better if she believed that he had tried to rape her. She should desert him. He pictured her once more in her flowing dress on the train with her long hair tossing in the breeze. She was so beautiful, so elegant, so intelligent. He had loved the girl he created in his mind who had become the heroine of his book. Valerie epitomized that mental vision of perfection. He could not help but love her too.

Claudia wiped the sweat from his forehead. "Are you comfortable now, Roby?"

"Yes, don't worry. I'm OK, but how about you?"

"I'm also OK. We must sustain each other. I feel sure that soon we will be free. Tell me about Valerie. I think she is a fantastic person and lovely too. How do you feel about her?"

"I'm sure you can imagine what a surprise it was to meet the girl I had created in my mind. I thought I would always have to close my eyes to picture her. Now that she is real, it is like a dream come true. I sometimes believe that I created her, then brought her to life. I envy our father spending peaceful time in her company. So far I haven't enjoyed that pleasure."

"How do you mean?" Claudia queried with surprise. "I understood that you met at the Blind Centre, surely there were no inhibitions there?"

"I must tell you the truth."

Roberto went on to explain exactly what had happened on the train.

Having heard all the details Claudia was very shocked. She knew and loved her brother dearly and had no hesitation in believing his story. Even so she could imagine how his actions must have appeared to Valerie, and could appreciate her reaction under the circumstances.

"It is just amazing to me," Claudia remarked, "that Valerie did not give the details to the police, she is obviously very intelligent and understanding."

They both became silent as they heard a car arriving in the courtyard below. Soon there came the sound of footsteps on the stairs followed by the door opening then Zdrazil entered the room. He had a quick conversation with the two guards, then turned his attention to the brother and sister.

"I must apologize for the inconvenience and discomfort. Unfortunately two hunters stumbled across the farm and we were obliged to inactivate them before they found you."

"You killed them," snapped Claudia.

"No, certainly not," replied Zdrazil.

"They were tied up. Then after you had been transferred the police were informed of their whereabouts. They were not harmed in any way. Tomorrow Valerie will join us here. In the meantime please make yourselves as comfortable as you can. Anything you need that we can offer will be made available. You simply have to tell the guard, he will be in the adjoining room. Now we will leave you. Have you eaten?"

"We had sandwiches at the farm, however, I think a bowl of soup would be good for my brother."

"Certainly. I will have my wife prepare some and bring it to you. Excuse me," Zdrazil responded. Then he and the guards left the room.

Roberto and Claudia were amazed at the courtesy they were being shown and began to relax, feeling confident that they would shortly be free. Roberto would then have the medical treatment he needed and there would be a joyous meeting with their father.

After half-an-hour Zdrazil's wife arrived with the soup. She had a very Austrian demeanor, though, like Zdrazil, she was presumably Slovak too. She was substantially built and the straps of her dress, which was tightly belted at the waist, cut into her broad shoulders. Her black, multilayered skirt had a rustic design, suggesting that she originated from the countryside. She handed Roberto a large bowl and mumbled something. From the tray she placed a further bowl on the table, while doing so she looked very fiercely directly into Claudia's eyes, then she left.

Following her departure the two agreed that they were glad to be in the care of Zdrazil rather than his wife

The soup was good and seemed to have a strong medicinal effect on Roberto, who, having consumed it quite rapidly, declared that he felt a great deal better.

Claudia expressed her relief that the blood she had first seen on his plaster cast had not originated from the wound to his leg. She had cleaned his facial wounds and applied band-aids and he certainly looked much better.

Now that they were more comfortable, Roberto sat up and smiled at his sister. He was very pleased to see her. They had not met for six months and even though they were not twins they were unusually close. Being one year older than he, she had had the responsibility of taking care of him when the nurse was not available, in addition to which she had been his eyes, and as such, had had considerable influence on his development. She had been his entire media for the first six years of his life until he began to learn Braille and all the other compensatory lessons devised for the blind.

As he now looked at her once more, he began to wonder whether it was her mind that had created Valerie for him. On recollection he had used her face by touch as reference. When he touched her hair and said that the girl of his dreams had longer hair and then gradually built up a picture by comparison with her face, maybe it was simply the need for the girl in the book to be different, that he described her the way he did.

Claudia was also beautiful and he was very proud of her. She had given up her youth to be at his side to protect him. He would always be indebted to her. Since he became sighted she had gone off to live the life she had missed. Each day had to be full of friends and lovers. She was not promiscuous but loved to be in love. Two months previously she had met Peter. He was very English, an

Oxford graduate, from a home with Victorian discipline which formed the background to his upbringing.

Claudia admired Peter for his promptness and reliability. It was almost like finding a young edition of her father. Roberto knew of Peter from their last telephone conversation, now with their long, relaxed talk he was able to gain more insight as to who Peter was. It was evident from the way Claudia spoke of him that she was very much in love with him.

She was also happy to have some time, once more, with her brother, though she began to worry for Peter. Once he realized that she was missing he would pursue every avenue until he found her. Nothing would stop him. She was sure that with his intelligence and ability, by now he would at least have traced her to Vienna. Fortunately he spoke fluent German and would be able to make his own enquiries at the airport.

Peter had been in her mind constantly since she left for Vienna, though the events of the past few days had so preoccupied her that she had not had the opportunity to consider Peter's potential actions. She would like to have told Roberto what was on her mind, but if Peter was going to suddenly walk through the door, she didn't want to say something that might be overheard and alert their captors.

What would Peter do? she contemplated. The day she left they had arranged to speak by telephone late in the evening. She had not called. She had not arrived at the hotel. The warning bells would have sounded for him. He wouldn't waste time waiting for a flight, rather he would jump into his beloved Ferrari and by early the following morning be in France. Certainly by evening he would have arrived at Vienna airport. There he would show her picture to the customs and passport officials. Schwechat airport was relatively small and Claudia knew that she would have been noticed. Everywhere she went she had admiring glances. Sometimes she longed to be inconsequential. Under the circumstances she hoped that someone at the airport might have information for Peter. Maybe he at least had confirmation that she had arrived in Vienna. She felt it was simply a matter of time.

At the hotel Valerie was so tired that, even with the events of the day, the Jacuzzi had soothed her sufficiently that once her head touched the pillow she quickly fell into a deep, relaxing sleep.

It was 8 a.m. the following morning when she awoke feeling quite refreshed. Her adrenalin began to flow immediately as she prepared herself with great anticipation for the 10 a.m. meeting. While she was applying the finishing touches to her make-up the telephone rang. It was the Baron, anxious to know that she had slept well and once again asking her to withdraw and take no further risks on behalf of his family. They would surely find another way to resolve the problems.

She pointed out that if she failed to go through with the arrangements, as dictated by Zdrazil, his children would be in great danger. She had lived through a situation far more terrifying than the current one. Maybe one day she would tell him. He begged her to take the greatest precautions and no risks whatsoever. The conversation closed with a request that she convey his love to his children and say that he was very anxious to see them as soon as possible.

The final meeting for the allocation of funds from the bank was scheduled for that day. For the moment he would do his best to follow the instructions of the group in the hope that whatever transpired might be rectified later.

At 10 a.m. sharp a knock on the door set Valerie's heart racing. She realized that it was not only due to the situation but also to the fact that she would soon be seeing Roberto once more. She longed for him. She also longed for the day when they would be together, when she could look into his eyes. Eyes were very important to them, both knowing what a vital gift was sight. He had beautiful eyes and she knew how he loved to look into her eyes. She pictured his strong face, his thick black hair. Even when she felt insecure, unsure of the story he had given to justify his action on the train, she still felt a strong desire to kiss him long and hard on the lips. He had well-formed lips and the first kiss was anticipated with joy. The warmth now flowing through her body was a mild anticipation of what was to come.

She opened the door, holding her white stick, and looked through Zdrazil. His black beret seemed to be part of him. It was there always. She was sure that if he knew she was able to see him he would remove it and tilt his head slightly forward in a salute. But he believed her to be blind, consequently the beret remained in place.

"Good morning, I trust you slept well," Zdrazil inquired.

"Thank you," she replied. "And you?"

He did not reply, maybe indicating that he had not. She recalled that last night, when he spoke on the car phone, he had become very agitated.

"Please come with me. We will join your friends."

It was not long after they left the hotel that Valerie realized they were not going toward the farm. Curious and frightened though this made her, she succeeded in refraining from making any observation.

This time the journey was much shorter. After only fifteen minutes the car turned into the courtyard of Zdrazil's house and came to a stop. Valerie heard the crunch of the gravel under the tires of the Mercedes, "I did not hear gravel yesterday and today's journey was shorter. Where are we?"

"Don't be alarmed. Yesterday evening we were obliged to move from the farm. We are at my house in Bratislava. Please come with me."

Zdrazil led her up the stairs and into the room where Claudia and Roberto were anxiously awaiting her. They greeted one another happily and with great relief while Zdrazil left the room saying that coffee would be brought to them shortly.

"How is our father?" Claudia asked.

"He is well, though very concerned for you both. He sent his love and said that he will do everything possible to ensure that no harm comes to us." As she spoke she sat on the bed and took Roberto's hand. In her hand she had already prepared a note in braille telling him in brief all that had transpired the previous evening.

Each of them scrutinized the room for any sign of a lens or microphone. Nothing was visible, though that was not conclusive. Even so, they imagined that with the quick transfer the previous evening, there had been little possibility to prepare monitoring equipment, in addition to which it probably would no longer be necessary. The message had been passed to the Baron and today was the final day of the committee meetings.

Coffee arrived, that very dense and distinct taste they were beginning to become accustomed to, then once more they were left to exchange experiences.

Claudia confessed her knowledge of the incident on the train and expressed her sincere sorrow at the suffering inadvertently inflicted upon Valerie by Roberto. She knew of her brother's obsession with the girl from his dream and although she was horrified at what had transpired on the train she was absolutely confident that he sincerely believed her to be a manifestation of the girl in his book and mind. She hoped that Valerie would give him the opportunity to prove himself.

"Do you still have the manuscript?" Roberto interjected.

"No," she replied. "It was taken to the hospital."

The Baron had had no sleep whatever and when reception called to tell him of the arrival of Peter, he felt a great sense of relief. Previously he had met Peter only once but took an instant liking to him on that occasion, consequently when he arrived at the suite the Baron welcomed him with open arms.

Peter was very pleased to have news of Claudia, having had little success at the airport. He spent many hours there questioning porters, police and finally the crew of the flight that had brought the girls to Vienna, fortunately they flew in while he was making his enquiries at the airport. The girls had been seen by several people but no one was able to give any precise information. Beyond the airport exit the trail died.

Claudia had mentioned that her father was in Bratislava; consequently he decided to drive there and see what information, if any, her father might have.

Information he certainly had, though it was not what Peter wanted to hear; however, it was a great relief to have some idea where she was and that she was alive and well. Karl had already called the VB, the local police in Bratislava. They had told him the story of the hunters who had been found at the farm. An inquiry had been instigated and so far it had been established that a black Mercedes had been seen coming and going at the farm, also a white Citröen, which had been traced and the owner was being held for questioning. The police were of the opinion that the events might be related.

With this new information and a great deal more confidence than when he originally set out for Vienna, Peter decided to call at VB headquarters. There, once more, his knowledge of the German language proved very useful. He was surprised how many officers spoke German, particularly the older ones.

With the information that he now added to the investigation a picture began to form. There was one very important factor that neither he nor the police had. That was the involuntary involvement of the Baron, who had decided against relating the intended theft of the World Bank loan.

The Baron went along to the meeting of the committee and, true to his word, he did his best to convince the committee that the greater part of the fund, set aside, should go to the Slovak Republic. His prime concern was the safety of the three captives. He had not intended to try to sway the committee that way because he felt that Slovakia would not necessarily be helped by a large injection of funds. It was his belief that the newly formed state needed to establish its government and infrastructure plan first, whereas the Czech Republic had been forging ahead in an extraordinary manner. The state had virtually no debt and the Czech crown had retained it's value over the previous three years. The Czech government may not even have accepted the offer that probably would have been allocated to them, without the compelling situation that now existed.

It was agreed that a sum of $270,000,000, over a three-year period, would be made available to the Slovak Republic, with an instant opening figure of $160,000,000. The national bank would be obliged to gain authority from the World Bank of Development and Reconstruction before advancing any figure in excess of $25,000,000.

The Baron felt a certain sense of relief on the decision. Presumably Zdrazil would access the maximum amount available, then he and his associates would be gone and the prisoners released.

He left the meeting initiating the count in his mind of the hours before he would be reunited with Roberto, Claudia and Valerie, following which he would immediately declare the full circumstances of the affair to the European Parliament in Brussels, in the hope that the money might be recovered.

The evening news carried the decision, on hearing which Zdrazil became very confident and excited.

He went through the plan in his mind. Tomorrow the director of the State bank would make the transfer to the twenty-five banks throughout Eastern Europe and the Middle East. One million dollars to each bank. Once that was completed he would meet up with Zdrazil and they would drive the eighty miles to Brno in the Czech Republic, their destination there being the container depot on the outskirts of that city. An occurrence that had taken place there four years previously was a key factor in the plan.

Zdrazil recalled the day he heard the story from the director of the container depot.

Toward the end of 1989 seventeen containers loaded with vodka arrived from Russia. Then came the Velvet Revolution, the event that was to indirectly facilitate their escape route.

In addition to major political repercussions, the bloodless *coup d'état* also affected many aspects of trade that had existed, undisturbed for the previous forty years. Following the collapse of that stable trade, when the account for the vodka arrived no one would accept responsibility for payment. The consequent return of the containers to Russia provided Zdrazil with the perfect method of leaving the country. Roads, airports, even railways would be controlled in an endeavor to apprehend the thieves but no one would think of goods to Russia.

The director of container transport had had ample time to prepare one of the containers. It would not be so uncomfortable, just about a six-hour journey, then they would be outside the Slovak Republic and so would the money.

Once inside Russia the group of eight would leave the container, drive south through Rumania and on to Sofia, in Bulgaria. There they would access the first million at the state bank, following which they would divide all the bank accounts amongst themselves, separate and go their own ways. Each had their own dreams of paradise.

SIX

It was 7 a.m. the following morning when Zdrazil burst into the room where the prisoners were being held. He was anxious to get moving. "Good morning, everyone. I have good news for you. Tomorrow you will be released. Valerie, I compliment you. Apparently you were sufficiently persuasive with the Baron."

This announcement came as a surprise to Valerie. The plan devised by Karl did not provide for such a speedy result and would no longer be effective. What could she do? She was pleased that tomorrow they would be free; however, the question of the many millions of dollars that would be stolen from the grant would reflect upon the integrity of the Baron.

The transmitter she was carrying was not even switched on so as to conserve the battery. She excused herself and went to the bathroom. There she switched on the miniature unit, then hurriedly returned to the other room. The question was would the transmission be monitored so early in the morning?

It was not enough. Other action was called for. She thought for a moment, then an idea occurred to her. "Mr.

Zdrazil, I think I lost an earring in the car on the journey here. Would you permit me to search for it? I am sure you are very busy with your preparations." Zdrazil pondered for a moment then called one of the guards to accompany Valerie to the Mercedes.

The guard took advantage of the opportunity to have a cigarette and left Valerie to search alone.

After a few moments, pretending to search around the seats of the car, Valerie succeeded in removing the transmitter from her bra and stuffing it under the back seat, she then held up the earring, that had been in her pocket all the time, and announced, "I've found it."

The driver accompanied Valerie as they returned to the room on the top floor, where Zdrazil expressed satisfaction that she had been successful in her search.

It was Monday morning. Valerie thought to herself that Karl might begin to monitor the device shortly. There would be nothing to hear; however, if or when the car moved maybe it would be possible to track it by the transmissions, subsequently giving some guide as to the whereabouts of Zdrazil, who now happily declared, "To celebrate the success of our mission, my wife will prepare a fine lunch for us all today and I hope you will join us downstairs in the dining room."

"Naturally if you do release us tomorrow, as you say, that will be a great relief, though I think I can speak for the three of us," Roberto stated, "when I say that we have no desire to celebrate your theft of the fund. You will be unimaginably rich, the people of the Slovak Republic will continue to be unimaginably poor. They are your countrymen. Do you have no feeling of remorse or concern for them?"

"I have no wish nor intent to involve myself in a discussion on ethics or right or wrong with you, Roberto.

You and your family have lived a privileged life and can have no conception of my life or that of my colleagues. You must excuse me now, your meals will be sent up to you. Good day."

Once a disappointed Zdrazil had left the room, Roberto and Claudia became depressed with the frustration of actually being there with the criminals and being unable to take any action that might at least delay them, until Valerie leaned across and whispered in Roberto's ear that she had succeeded in planting a transmitter in the Mercedes, then gave the same information to Claudia.

The satisfaction with Valerie's act caused Roberto to remark on her resourcefulness and the conversation began to revolve around her and her background. Claudia picked up a magazine and settled herself on the couch for the final period of their captivity.

Valerie had accepted Roberto's explanation of the events on the train and she began to feel very sorry and concerned for the severe wound she had inflicted upon him.

For his part Roberto, now fully aware of how his actions had appeared to Valerie, had an enormous desire to demonstrate his sincere remorse.

Valerie took his hand and looked deeply into his eyes. The contact of flesh and mind was so intense that great restraint was necessary to refrain from further contact.

Roberto took advantage of the first real possibility to look deeply into Valerie's eyes. He knew that she had beautiful eyes, though before this moment he had not had the opportunity to concentrate deeply on them. Now he could see just how beautiful they were. Deep green with just a hint of brown. Open fully to the world and clear, so very clear and sparkling, just as he had imagined.

"We have never confirmed the exact date that I lost my sight and you gained yours," Valerie said. "The dates will be engraved upon our minds for completely opposite reasons. For me it was September 10th, 1992."

"That is quite incredible," Roberto replied. "That is the exact day that I opened my eyes in the morning and believed that I was dreaming. The event astounded all the experts at the Blind Centre. When I was born my parents were told there was no possibility that I would ever see. When I did become sighted it was made even more extraordinary by the fact that it was both eyes that sprang into life simultaneously. Until that moment I had been a curiosity with my insistence that I constantly dreamed with clear images in my mind. No one believed me."

"The day you saw for the first time," Valerie asked. "Did you have confirmation of your dreams? Did you then see in reality what had previously been images in your mind? Or is it possible that Claudia had been instrumental in convincing you that what was in your mind was what sighted people saw."

"I must confess that the mass of information that suddenly flooded into my brain, the day I first saw, was so overwhelming that I can no longer be sure. I continued to have dreams that I felt were the same as those I had experienced while still blind but if I am realistic about it, it is surely impossible for an actual picture to appear in the mind of one who has never seen before and therefore has nothing to relate to."

"Because of what transpired before the train crash, hate and anger were in my mind," Valerie confessed. "When my head received the blow that triggered my eyes back into full function, although the anger and hate were still there, once I saw you, I had the extraordinary feeling that I wanted to be with you. Common sense told me what I should do. My heart told me that I loved you. How could an intelligent person believe the notation of a heart that gave such ridiculous, contradictory messages? I fought and fought my feelings but on each occasion that I had the possibility to denounce you, words came out of my mouth that did not seem to originate from my brain. I began to think that I was schizophrenic, seeming to be under two totally different commands. Whenever I wished to follow my logical conclusions I acted quite differently."

"Valerie, tell me truly. Can you honestly believe that I would rape anyone, that I would even harm or cause fear?"

"No, I believe you," she replied with great sincerity.

At that moment they could resist no longer. Valerie drew closer and closer until their lips touched. That first contact sent a rippling sensation down both their spines, a ripple that became warm on its return. It was as though their beings joined together in one. Neither wanted to withdraw, they had waited so long. The previous week, with all the remarkable occurrences, had seemed like a year.

He placed his hand gently on the nape of her neck, ran his fingers over the perfect round of the back of her head, then through her long auburn hair.

Claudia had heard all that had been said. The demonstration of feelings so deep caused her no embarrassment. She was pleased her brother should be privileged with such a powerful love. Their actions were simply a natural progression of feelings releasing themselves in acts of love.

As Roberto's hands arrived at the ends of Valerie's hair he gathered the whole length and crushed it gently in a circular motion on her head. Neither one closed their eyes. They were both experiencing something wonderful and wanted to drink in the beauty of their eyes and see deep into each other's minds, to see there the marvel of love. This was the first touch but for both it seemed as though they had touched always.

The pressure of the kiss became more gentle and Valerie allowed her lips to drift over his face and down the side of his neck. There she kissed him once more, then withdrew, remembering that Claudia was there in the room with them.

As they drew apart Claudia suddenly began to applaud in an involuntary action, then realizing what she was doing the clap became irregular, then ceased.

"What am I doing?" she said. "I was just so delighted to see you both in love and so happy that, once the action was sealed with a kiss, it appeared to me as the finale of a wonderful play. Please excuse me, I should have given you your privacy. I confess that I just could not resist what I saw and heard."

Valerie and Roberto each held out a hand to Claudia and smiled with their eyes full of joy.

Each was gaining new knowledge of the other and the time passed pleasantly. In different circumstances and surroundings, with the normal pressure of life they may not have had the possibility to get to know each other so profoundly. Consequently there was one good aspect to their situation.

Evening came and the meal Zdrazil had promised arrived. His wife had prepared a traditional Slovak recipe. Three large plates were brought into the room and set upon the table. First a very large dumpling that had been precut into half inch slices, then a substantial heap of steaming sauerkraut, finally pork tenderloin that had also been sliced, with rich juices ladled over the top.

The three could not help but anticipate with pleasure the certain titillation of their taste buds, an extraordinary reaction considering that they were being held as hostages.

Zdrazil prepared three beautiful, delicate, oval, porcelain plates, each with two slices of meat, two slices of dumpling and a generous ladle of sauerkraut. The plates thus prepared, he served the prisoners, assuring them that they could return as often as they desired. He then left the room and shortly returned with six bottles of finest Pilzen beer, explaining that Pilzen is a city in the west of the Czech Republic and is the name from which Pils, Pilsen and all other variations of that particular lager beer originate.

"Thank you," followed Zdrazil's exit as he left to enjoy the same meal with his wife and the two guards in the dining room downstairs.

None of the three had eaten that particular meal before and the fact that it was home cooked and prepared added much to the memorable experience. The beer was, in itself, a treat, creating as it did a perfect accompaniment to a simple but delightful meal.

It was perhaps thirty minutes after eating that peaceful drowsiness overcame them. It felt quite natural to Valerie to lift her feet onto the bed where Roberto lay, rest her head beside his and before a gentle kiss could even be completed, fall asleep beside him.

Claudia had already succumbed. The room was warm, in contrast to the frosty air of an early touch of winter that began the process of tinging the trees with silvery white tips.

Satisfied stomachs, warmth and a certain fatigue from talking all day permitted their surrender to sleep with no resistance. There had been an additional ingredient in the meal, of which they had not been aware. It had not affected the taste in any way, though it had a substantial effect in facilitating their sleep, a sleep that persisted for about ten hours.

A sudden buzz of activity jolted the trio back from their slumbers. They concentrated their attention on their ears and heard the sound of several cars arriving and braking violently.

Then there was someone calling, "Claudia, Claudia, where are you? Are you all right?" Claudia's eyes lit up and she exclaimed excitedly, "It's Peter!"

Now came the opportunity for Valerie and Roberto to witness love on the face of Claudia.

"Peter, I am here, upstairs, third floor."

Each then realized that they had not been aware of sound for some time before. Another thing that occurred to them was that they had all slept unusually deeply and long that night, then came the realization that they had been administered some sort of sleeping drug, perhaps they should have suspected what presented itself as a last supper.

Certainly they had been receiving treatment that would not normally be associated with being held hostage. No doubt the kindness constituted part of the overall plan, lulling them, as it did, into a false sense of security.

They presumed that Zdrazil had probably left and they were right.

The sound of footsteps, leaping two or three stairs at a time, became more and more pronounced, then the door swung open and Peter stood there. His entrance seemed somehow corny, resembling the arrival of Indiana Jones. He invariably wore track suits and this was an occasion that lent itself to such an attire. Valerie and Roberto saw him for the first time. He was tall, about six feet, with crew cut hair, broad shoulders and strong hands exposed at the sleeves of his suit. Claudia imagined that he had left for Vienna exactly as he now appeared. She jumped up, ran to him and they embraced long and tenderly.

His entry was quickly followed by officers of the VB and there ensued many unanswered questions. Despite the jokes directed at the VB by the Czech and Slovak people the detective following this investigation was no fool. He knew that there had been an attempt on the life of the Baron. He knew that Roberto and Claudia were the son and daughter of the Baron. Where Valerie fitted in was not clear.

The three decided not to speak of the robbery of the fund until they had spoken to the Baron.

The detective posed many questions but still could not discover any reason for kidnapping or attempted murder. Valerie put forward the proposition that it may be connected with the European farming subsidies, following what she had been told by the Baron.

The detective was not happy. He went on to tell them that the police had discovered that Zdrazil had bought six tickets to Rio, leaving from Vienna. The flight had already left, consequently they would now have to wait until the aircraft landed. The police then expected, with the cooperation of the Brazilian police, to pick up Zdrazil and his accomplices.

He instructed that the four of them should make themselves available for further questioning then left.

In the meantime an ambulance arrived to take Roberto to hospital. Valerie went with the ambulance and agreed to join the other two later at the hotel, where they would go to speak to Claudia's father.

Roberto was very frustrated by his immobility but agreed that Valerie should join the other two. The priority now was somehow to locate the stolen money. As she left Valerie promised that whatever happened she would keep in constant touch.

The foyer of the hotel was a hive of activity on her arrival. Somehow the press had some indication of what was going on and were buzzing around like dogs on a scent.

It was all the hotel staff could do to restrain them from reaching the suite of the Baron.

Valerie managed to squeeze through the throng and was allowed passage. She bypassed her own room and went directly to that of the Baron. They were all pleased to meet up once more and Valerie assured the Baron that his son was comfortable and on the way to a full recovery.

Karl had traced the Mercedes, with the aid of the transmitter, to the container depot. There the trail ended. The police had also been there, but had disregarded the possibility of that eventuality being related to the escape route, considering it a decoy and favoring the exit by air to Rio as being more logical.

Peter put forward the premise that it was the air tickets that constituted the decoy, being rather obvious. The others agreed and decided that they should get to the container depot as quickly as possible.

During the afternoon the Baron would be flying to Brussels, where he had an appointment with the director of the Bank of Development and Reconstruction. He intended to give full details of the theft and his involuntary participation. He had not given the information to the local police. That would be the decision of Brussels.

Peter, Claudia and Valerie drove to Brno and located the container depot beside the Brno-Ostrava highway. The black Mercedes was visible as soon as they entered the yard. It was being guarded by two policemen who completely lost interest in their charge with the arrival of the Ferrari. They wandered across fixated on the car and paying no attention to the occupants, who quickly got out and left the policemen to ogle while they entered the depot building.

The receptionist spoke neither English nor German and in a show of embarrassment called the deputy director to her aid, who spoke a little of both.

Peter came straight to the point and asked to see the records of departures for the last couple of days. He was told that the director was the only one authorized to make that sort of information available. Then, having given the matter considerable thought, the deputy director decided that in the absence of the director, which was the situation that day, he automatically became the chief, in which capacity and fluffing up with his own importance, he agreed to open the books and assist in any way he could.

Whilst they scanned the information, the deputy director, who was a very jovial character, told them the story of a Czech man who called at the depot wishing to arrange transportation of his belongings to Russia. His request was so strange that all the employees, on hearing of it, came to have a look at the man, thinking that he must be mentally retarded. Six months after arriving in Russia the man telephoned to say that winter was approaching and he had still not received the goods, which included his winter clothing. He was advised that the container had been sitting just inside the Russian border for the previous six months.

Coinciding with the completion of the story, Peter arrived at the entry concerning the seventeen containers of vodka. The story he had just heard may have been a thought for Zdrazil's logic. No one voluntarily goes to Russia and no one expects that anyone else would either. Rio would be a far more obvious choice.

The possibility that they had left for Russia began to have credence and the four agreed that they must trace the containers.

The time of departure of the load suggested that it would just about have arrived inside the Russian border. Try though he may the deputy director was unable to make either telephone or telex contact with the border station.

There was no time to lose. The three tendered their thanks and hurried to where the policemen were still mesmerized by the magnificent lines of the Ferrari. They would have to return to the job of guarding the Mercedes because the three quickly boarded the car and set off for Chop, the customs railway depot, just inside the Russian border.

Study of the map suggested that the 500km direct overland route would be very slow. They therefore headed for Bratislava. The 110km journey was completed in thirty-eight minutes, necessitating a speed very much in excess of the legal limit.

The next leg, to Budapest, could not be travelled so quickly. There was much more traffic and several police cars in evidence.

On arrival at the magnificent city astride the Danube, they decided to stop for a quick meal. By then it was late evening and they were all hungry. It was also necessary to call Roberto and the Baron to bring them up to date on their progress.

The Hungarian cellar restaurant served them with goulash, in miniature witches' cauldrons slung beneath tripods. There was no Gypsy music to accompany their meal, just the loud hum of a huge refrigerator that seemed intent on going into orbit, judging by its violent and erratic movements.

Little time was lost eating and once the telephone calls were completed they hurriedly left the restaurant and the half eaten goulash, taking the road north to Miskolc, from there east to Nyiregyhaza, then finally the last section north to the Russian border crossing.

It was 3 a.m. when they finally arrived at Chop where language once again proved to be a problem, until the border guards located one of their officers by telephone who spoke a sort of English. He was very helpful and put them in contact with the rail customs police at Mukachevo.

The train had arrived and it had already been discovered that one of the containers was empty and had a hole cut in the floor.

The customs officers had been making their own enquiries and had discovered that two cars, previously parked near the station for several days, were no longer there. A description of the cars had been circulated and a report had already been received that the cars had entered Rumania at 4 a.m..

SEVEN

The Ferrari arrived at Satu Mare, the first major town in Rumania, around 6 a.m. It was cold, due to a Föhn wind that descended without mercy from the Carpathian mountains. Valerie had been sleeping a little, despite the cramped conditions in the back of the Ferrari, while Peter drove slowly around the sleepy town looking for a police station or some early riser who might possibly speak English, German or Italian. They speculated that as Rumanian language is Latin-based, maybe Italian would be understood.

"Stop," cried Valerie. Peter, fearing some problem, effected an immediate emergency stop, then turned to Valerie.

"Please go back about 100 metres." Peter obeyed the request then turned once more to Valerie. "Look, that tree, I know it, I've seen it before, it must mean something."

Peter looked at Claudia who asked Valerie, "What do you mean? How could you know that particular tree? Surely you have never been here before?"

"No, of course not. The shape of that tree appeared, exactly as we see it, in the condensed water vapor on the faucet of the Jacuzzi at the hotel in Bratislava."

"Excuse my skepticism," Peter said cynically. "I have only just met you. You must appreciate that what you are saying is a little far-fetched."

"Peter, if Valerie has a feeling about that tree, then I for one am happy to consider what significance it may have. Let's just look around here for a while."

The relationship was too new for Peter to comment any further and he kept quiet with the other two as they slowly scanned in all directions, looking for they knew not what.

The dead tree stood on the corner of a small side street. There was nothing else, no building, nothing. Without a word Peter turned the car and began to enter the side street. He had driven just forty or fifty yards when, on the right-hand side of the road, a house came into view. A big elegant-looking mansion, quite out of place in that part of the world.

They were just able see, over the top of the high hedge that surrounded the house, two cars parked at the front entrance.

"Those were the cars used by Zdrazil and his associates," Valerie whispered confidently. Peter opened the glove compartment and took out a small pistol.

"No," whispered Claudia. "We know that Zdrazil may have the two guards with him. I have been thinking throughout our journey, you remember that the director of the container depot was absent when we called there yesterday morning? He may be one of the group. Also how about the money? Surely a senior official of the state bank is involved and what about this house? It is not an hotel. Zdrazil probably has contacts here too. That makes at least six of them.

"That's right," Peter agreed. "Like us they are probably tired. We surely have some time in hand. I suggest that you two girls take the Ferrari and look for a police station. I'll stay here and keep an eye on the two cars. By the way, Valerie, please forgive my doubting you. I don't understand, but I'm definitely impressed."

It was agreed. Valerie and Claudia set off to look for the police station. Driving away they glanced back, Peter looked very cold and lonely. The car backed slowly and as quietly as possible out of the road, turned and drove in the direction of the town centre. Fortunately they found the police station quite quickly and Claudia, who had been driving, parked the car. They got out and went into the building, which looked as dilapidated as all the others they had seen since arriving in the town.

A very unpleasant looking man, in uniform, was sleeping across two wooden chairs. His belt was unbuckled and his huge beer belly bulged, looking both satisfied and revolting. He was not pleased to be disturbed and snapped something unrecognizable. Valerie meekly asked, "Do you speak English?" His reply was evidently no. Claudia tried, "Parla italiano?" Again no apparent recognition.

On a table Valerie noticed a pen and paper. She beckoned the policeman and walked toward the desk. He grumbled something but joined her there. Valerie wrote, 'Police U.S.S.R., Mukachevo, 2 auto.' This time his response was positive. He nodded in the affirmative, walked to a door at the back of the office, knocked and went in, closing the door behind him.

It was only a couple of minutes before a handsome officer with a large black moustache came from the office, the unpleasant one following.

"I England speak."

"You speak English?" responded Valerie, with a certain amount of doubt.

"Of course. You car Mukachevo?"

"No," Valerie responded and reverted to the paper once more, having little confidence that the officer had a high command of the English language.

On the paper she drew, from memory, a map of the location of the house and marked a cross to indicate its position, then wrote, '2 auto.'

"Very good, we go here, OK?"

Valerie reverted to the paper once more, thinking it important that he be prepared for a potential confrontation, she wrote 'eight/ten men.'

"Many man, understand, I speak good England. Yes?"

"Yes, you speak good England."

He shouted some precise sounding commands to the unpleasant one, who saluted and left the room. Then he went to the telephone and began making calls, probably to Russia.

Valerie and Claudia could only speculate as to what was going on and pray that soon they would be returning to the house and Peter, who must be very cold by now. They were not prepared for such conditions and he was wearing only his famous track suit.

Soon the unpleasant one reappeared, this time with six others dressed in very untidy, dirty uniforms. They carried rifles and looked like a bunch of criminals themselves. The chief completed his telephone calls, whipped his wild bunch into some sort of order, then led everyone out of the police station.

There were three vehicles standing in front of the building that had not been there before. The chief indicated that Claudia should go with the unpleasant one, in an open top, Russian jeep, then he directed Valerie to the Ferrari.

"Beautiful Italian auto, you auto?"

"No, friend auto, he at house."

She drove, leading the way back to the house, where, on arrival, she stopped short, as on the previous occasion. Peter had heard the vehicles approaching and was walking toward them. To the police chief Peter was a stranger in town and he reached for his revolver. Valerie, noticing his action, touched his arm and in subdued tones said, "He friend auto." The chief seemed to understand and replaced his weapon.

Everyone left the vehicles and grouped in front of the chief like a collection of boy scouts awaiting instructions.

Poor Claudia was frozen and under the circumstances Peter was unable to warm her, though the excitement of the moment tended to mask their state of body temperature. They stood back with Valerie as the chief organized his rabble who then began to move into position around the house. By now it was after 7 a.m. and beginning to get light. There appeared to be some hope of a sunny day. The sky was clear and the ghost of the half moon was about to go to Austria.

Once his men were in place the chief and his next in command walked casually up to the front door of the house and knocked. The door was soon opened and after a few moments they went in.

Peter, Claudia and Valerie remained on the pavement with their gaze firmly fixed on the house. They saw a curtain being slightly opened, then quickly closed. Peter decided they were rather exposed, and walked back to the Ferrari where he took his revolver from the glove compartment.

It seemed doubtful there was any way that Zdrazil and his group could escape. They would have to run, but the house provided the only cover, with the exception of one other small house on the other side of the road and there were very few trees. Soon the chief came to the front door and beckoned the three to come to the house. They obeyed his instructions and walked up the steps to the front door.

"Come, come." The chief invited them to enter a large reception room at the foot of a massive, carved-wood staircase. In the room was a variety of people, all in their night attire, hair in disorder and looking very frightened. Amongst them stood Zdrazil whose look of fright turned to disbelief when he saw Peter, Claudia and Valerie entering the room in front of the chief. He realized immediately that Valerie had no white stick and moved and looked as a sighted person.

"Your act was very convincing," he said, looking at her with a smile that incorporated both admiration and disappointment.

"Everybody silent," commanded the officer, then he spoke to the unpleasant one who left once more.

Everyone did remain silent, respecting the order of the officer who moved slowly around the room, lifting each piece of china or ornament and studying it very carefully. One statuette appeared to be gold and for a moment it seemed unlikely that it would be replaced but the officer seemed to reconsider and gently set it back in its original position, as he did so turning to one old man and grinning. He, they thought, was probably the owner of the house.

The group included several middle-aged ladies, one they instantly recognized as the wife of Zdrazil. Amongst the others were probably the wives of the bank manager, container depot director, and one younger than the others who was possibly the wife of the owner of the house. She had dark hair and wore a lacy negligee and nightdress. Somehow she looked more at home than the others.

The police chief's mental cataloging of the expensive looking *objet d'art* proceeded until, after approximately fifteen minutes, his second in command returned, the cheeks of his face puffed up and bright red from apparently having been running. He spoke to the chief, a series of separated words, interspersed with the exhalation of mist from the cold air in his lungs. The chief then issued a further order that resulted in the calling of the other 'policemen' from outside the house.

Once all were gathered they each took control of one or two of the prisoners and led them from the room. Valerie, Claudia and Peter, following, observed that there was a small bus with barred windows parked in front of the house. The sorry line filed into the bus, then the police chief turned to Valerie and said, "Everyone to police station."

It appeared that the matter was now at an end and the three, on their return to the car, were suddenly hit by the fact that they had not slept for twenty-four hours; however, it was necessary to go to the police station, though they did hope that they might convince the police chief to permit them to have breakfast and to sleep before the inevitable interrogation began.

Back at the police station two additional cars had arrived, big Volgars, Russian limousines. Alongside each one a driver stood guard, occasionally flicking specks of dust from the dull paint work.

Inside confusion began as the population began to exceed the potential capacity of the room. The police chief shouted angrily, then turned to the three and repeated his orders in English, "Everyone silent." He justified his rank by his ability to gain immediate response to any command he issued and when two men appeared from the inner office, looking like SS, he revelled in that fact, as he stepped forward to meet them.

Valerie wondered to herself if they might be KGB but dismissed the idea after considering the cooling of relations between the two countries.

It seemed that their desire for rest was unlikely to be fulfilled, until one of the officials moved toward them and said in very good English, "I would like to thank you, on behalf of the Rumanian government, for your assistance in the apprehension of these dangerous, international terrorists. As far as we are concerned you may now leave, though I suggest that you return to the Slovak Republic, as I understand the VB wish to interview you."

Valerie took it upon herself to act as spokeswoman. "We thank you but may I ask? The three of us have had no sleep and we are hungry. Is there a hotel in this town where we might find comfortable accommodation?"

"Madam, my name is Colonel Rotaru of the Rumanian Intelligence Agency. I am not a tourist agent. Now if you will excuse me I have many important matters to attend to."

Valerie replied with a simple "Good day," turned to her friends and said, "Shall we go?"

Despite a mixture of anger and disappointment at the rebuff and ungracious attitude displayed toward them they silently left, thinking that the best course of action, whilst they had the possibility.

Once back in the car they sat for a few moments without speaking. Peter was first to break the silence.

"I suggest that we concentrate on finding an hotel. The important thing is that the thieves have been arrested and hopefully the money will be recovered."

"Agreed," said Valerie.

"Agreed," said Claudia. The car moved away in the direction of the town center.

By then it was 11:30 and there was a certain amount of activity on the streets. Sad thin horses pulled heavy farm carts. Cars that appeared to have been rescued from scrap yards moved in defiance of their condition and age.

After driving a mile or so the number of buildings and people suggested that they had arrived at the center of the town, though there were very few shops in evidence. The sun had risen but did little to breathe beauty or happiness into the scene. On a corner they saw what appeared to be a café. Peter parked the car, which was instantly surrounded by a throng of young people, excited and revering the three as though they must be celebrities to have such a beautiful car. Having entered the café, Peter held up a dollar, three fingers and ordered, "Coffee." The young woman behind the counter had difficulty in preparing the coffee, being reluctant to take her eyes from the dollar bill. She slid the dirty cracked cups of grey brown liquid along the counter and grabbed the dollar. Then from under the counter produced some very unappetizing looking rolls, filled with some kind of meat. Peter once more held up three fingers, she held out her hand, he produced another dollar, the hand remained still, he opened his wallet and offered another but before she could take it he held out his hand for the plate of rolls. He must have given the impression that that was the last dollar he was prepared to offer.

She passed the plate and took the money.

Following their first experience of bargaining in Rumania, they noticed a small back room, filled with smoke, and thinking that there might be some heat, moved into that heavy atmosphere. It was a degree or two less cold there, probably due to the body heat of half a dozen men sitting and smoking incessantly.

The conversation that had been in progress ceased and the locals all turned their attention to the new arrivals. One of them asked, "American?" Peter replied that they were English.

The man, who had a look of intelligence, crossed to where they now sat and asked if he might be of some assistance. Peter replied that they needed an hotel or somewhere to rest, as they had been travelling all night.

The helpful new acquaintance explained that there had been an hotel before 1948 but it had been taken over as the headquarters of the communist party. Tourists never came and there really was no need for an hotel in such a town.

He went on to say that his father had a very large house and he was sure they would be comfortable there. Peter gratefully accepted on behalf of the three and with their new guide they left the depressing café and returned to the car.

"Oh, that is wonderful. I have a passion for sports cars and love Ferrari. It is a 330GTC, I believe. My ancestors were part Italian and I have also learned to speak that language. Please allow me to introduce myself, my name is Georges Rotaru." The coincidence was extraordinary, they should be cautious. He was probably related to the secret service agent and could cause them more harm than good.

Without having the opportunity to discuss the potential risk, the three seemed to silently agree not to comment that they had heard the name previously and simply shook his hand in turn, while announcing their names. Peter also confirmed that the model of his car was indeed a 330GTC.

Now four were obliged to compress themselves into the Ferrari.

Peter followed the directions given him by Georges.

They hadn't travelled far before they began to realize that they were retracing their previous journey. They were soon to have an even bigger surprise because their final destination was the last they expected. Rotaru took them straight to the house with the big hedge on the small street by 'Valerie's tree.'

The surprise was such that they became dumbfounded and no one could begin to comment. They simply followed Georges up to the front door.

He opened the door and went in, calling his family. There was, of course, no reply.

"I don't understand, my parents are always home." Still no one spoke. "Excuse me one moment." He left them while he went to search the empty house, returning very soon. This time before he could speak Peter confessed, "We were here earlier today with the police. Your parents have been arrested. Excuse us for not speaking before, we were just so surprised."

"Zdrazil," exclaimed Georges. "He is the problem. I knew it when my father first spoke of him. I hadn't met him and knew nothing of him, I just knew that he was trouble. From the time my father met him he talked of nothing else. We will be rich, he said. You will go to Italy as you always dreamed. But why would we be rich? Just for providing accommodation for two days? I guessed that it involved something illegal." He spoke faster and more angrily. "My father would not have it. He said that our house is very important, an historic treasure and that this man Zdrazil was a Czech film director who was working for a German film company. Our house would be the perfect background to a film that was to be directed by Zdrazil."

Valerie now mentioned that they were surprised to hear the name Rotaru twice in one day.

"So you have met Colonel Rotaru, my cousin. He is the black sheep of the family. I would disown him if I could. Please tell me where you fit into this story."

Valerie gave him a brief resumé of what had happened, stressing the fact that they had been driving all day and night and suggesting that if it were possible they would very much like to have some sleep, following which they would be happy to tell him anything he wanted to know.

Georges accepted their explanation of what had happened without hesitation. He was obviously very shrewd.

"Forgive me, I am sure you can understand that I am rather shocked. Please allow me to show you to the bedrooms. You may select whichever you find most comfortable." As he led them up the stairs he continued, "I imagine you are surprised that I do not go instantly to the police station. I know these people and I know there is nothing that I could say or do that would be of any help at this stage. On the contrary, if I did go the problem might be compounded. The fact is that I would certainly be arrested myself if I went there. When I learn the full circumstances from you tomorrow, I will reconsider and see if there is a way that my parents could be helped."

The first room they passed was a bathroom, which he indicated was at their disposal, then on to the bedrooms.

When Valerie awoke she was surprised to find that it was six the following morning. She was amazed that she had slept so long; apparently the events of the previous forty-eight hours had made her very tired. Then as her mind became more active after her long sleep, the details of a very strange dream, she had experienced, began to filter back to her. The more she remembered the more she became anxious to relate the details to everyone.

Having taken a very welcome shower she went downstairs and was surprised to find Georges busy in the kitchen. "Good morning. I trust you slept well," he wished with a cheerful voice.

"Very well, thank you."

"I thought you must be hungry and have prepared a breakfast for you all. Everything is ready. Perhaps you would care to ask your friends to come to the table."

"That is very kind of you, we are certainly very hungry. Excuse me, I will call them."

Valerie went to the room where Claudia and Peter were just beginning to stir and informed them that a meal was awaiting them downstairs.

It was only half an hour later that all four were sitting in the spacious dining room and enjoying a breakfast of sausages, bacon, eggs, toast and marmalade together with English tea. Everyone agreed that it was most enjoyable and complimented Georges on his ability to create such a traditional English breakfast. He explained that most Rumanians have just a fresh green pepper for breakfast, or something equally simple.

The quality of the meal, together with the fact that they had not eaten for almost twenty-four hours, had the effect of creating an atmosphere, almost religious, at the table. Each one concentrated on the business of eating and limited the conversation to the bare minimum. When they had all finished eating Georges offered coffee in the sitting room, which they accepted with pleasure.

They went through to the same room where, the previous day, they had experienced seeing the arrest of the group, including Georges parents. Each wondered how the time had been for those now in prison.

Georges arrived with a silver tray on which were four small cups of dense Italian coffee. At this point Valerie gained the attention of everyone and asked for their patience while she related the dream she had experienced.

The dream commenced with a flight in a helicopter. Initially there were only herself and Claudia. Then she remembered turning once more and finding that they were no longer in the front. Georges was flying with Peter alongside him. The helicopter was very unstable, swinging in wide arcs from left to right and she saw smoke emitting from the rotor above. Then the scene suddenly changed. They were all tied up in an old barn and the smoke that had previously emitted from the area of the rotor of the helicopter, was now in clouds at the roof of the barn.

She remembered looking down and seeing her white stick protruding from a rope that was tied around her waist, then the dream ended and she woke up.

No one laughed, or made derogatory remarks. Peter and Claudia had witnessed an example of one of Valerie's visions and respected what she had to say. Then Georges began to speak.

"There is something significant about your dream which you could not possibly have known. The Russians operated a helicopter base on the outskirts of this town. I was employed as an engineer there. Then three years ago they finally left, taking all their equipment with them. The only thing that remained was one old helicopter that had crashed. They considered it beyond repair.

"I have spent the past three years working on it and just three weeks ago flew it for the first time. The question is, what does it mean?"

They all became troubled by the dream, then Georges asked that they tell him all they knew of the circumstances surrounding the arrest of his parents.

When the story was completed Georges said he felt it necessary to go to the police station. He did not trust his cousin and was concerned for his parents, who had been misled and become involved in something they would not have entertained had they known the truth.

"They are good people," he said, "and would certainly not break the law intentionally."

The three offered to accompany him to the police station, despite the rebuff of the previous morning, an offer Georges was delighted to accept.

As they came out of the house they were shocked to find that not only the two cars used by Zdrazil had been taken, but also the Ferrari was no longer there. Georges said that he had heard activity outside the house during the night and had seen the police taking the two cars but had not realized they had also taken the Ferrari.

"Now I am very concerned," he said. "My cousin is up to no good."

Being without any form of transport they were obliged to walk to the police station. They maintained a good pace for the short distance, being encouraged to move quickly by the low temperature of the still relatively early morning.

On arrival at the police station they discovered firstly there was no one in the outer office, then when they went into the room at the back, from where the officer with the moustache had come the previous day, a scene confronted them that gave some indication of the state of mind of Georges' cousin and his colleague.

The entire group from the house were tied and gagged and their hands were secured with one large rope that had then been attached to a ring affixed to the ceiling. They had no possibility of moving. On the floor, in large pools of blood, lay the unpleasant one and the police chief. Each had their throats cut. On being confronted with such a scene the two girls ran outside the building and vomited. Peter had witnessed such horror before and Georges succeeded in suppressing his feelings. They immediately began to free the others.

The women had been crying and appeared to have aged by ten years in the twenty-four hour period since they last saw them. They said nothing, just cuddled one another and wept.

The men, as they were freed, were anxious to relate the events of the previous twenty-four hours.

Zdrazil interrupted the proceedings. He had decided that his situation was impossible and his new concern was that Colonel Rotaru and his colleague be stopped.

The two girls returned to the room, taking care not to look in the direction of the bodies on the floor.

"My dear ladies," Zdrazil gained their attention. "I cannot possibly turn back the clock. My fate is sealed but I implore you to recover the money and return it to the Slovak government."

Valerie looked at Zdrazil's face as he spoke and saw once more that look of shame. He had been the cause of everything, even so she could not help but feel a certain sympathy for him. He had stolen money, that was obviously wrong, even so from the beginning he had behaved like a gentleman.

"What must we do?" Valerie questioned.

"Colonel Rotaru threatened the lives of the ladies, having first murdered the policemen as an indication of his sincerity. I couldn't stand by and see anyone else hurt so I gave him all the details of the transfer of funds to the twenty-five banks in Eastern Europe and the Middle East. The matter is complicated. I will give you all the information, then you must pursue them immediately. I am sure that they will go to Sofia first. At the central bank there, they will withdraw the $1,000,000 and from there begin the circuit of banks until they have the entire sum. Presumably they will then divide the sum and make their own arrangements on where to locate the money."

Mr. Sovicek, the director of the state bank in Bratislava, interjected at this point and had a surprise for everyone.

"I took the precaution of imposing two codes for each account," he said. "Rotaru has only one of those codes, believing that he has all the information necessary." He then turned to Zdrazil, "Forgive me, Miroslav. I felt it better that I maintain some method of protection, should you become greedy. Now I am glad that I did, though I regret having deceived you."

Now Peter had something to say.

"It appears to me that, with the exception of the owner of the house, each of you were involved in the crime and will have to face the consequences, regardless of whether you would or would not have harmed anyone. I am now going to telephone the British Embassy in Bucharest to request that they urgently arrange for police to be sent here to take charge of you. Once that has been achieved we will set off in pursuit of Rotaru and his associate."

"I fear that you will lose too much time," Zdrazil warned. "You are quite correct that Mr. Botosani, the owner of the house, knew nothing of our plans. I am afraid that I misled a good man and caused him suffering. May I suggest that you leave us in the charge of Mr. Botosani. It is necessary for him to see that we are brought to justice, in order to clear his own name, in which cause we will assist in any way we can."

The three looked at each other, then at Georges, who said, "You may trust my father completely. He will ensure that the group is taken into custody. You may take me as security against that fact. The other thing is that we do not have the Ferrari, they do. The Volgar in front of the police station, that was previously used by my cousin, would have no chance of catching the Ferrari; however, my helicopter is airworthy, though a little untidy. Let us go and follow the road to Sofia."

The three sensed the urgency and felt somehow that it was their duty to find Rotaru and his partner. They nodded in agreement to each other.

"We agree," Peter said. "Let's hurry."

EIGHT

The Volgars were still parked in front of the police station. It would have been reassuring to know the fate of the drivers who had been there earlier. Maybe they had been released from duty or maybe they had suffered the same fate as the two policemen. Time did not permit them to consider any further.

They hurried to the first car and found that the keys were still in the ignition, not that Georges appeared to be concerned either way. If he could rebuild a helicopter a car without ignition keys would surely present no problem. He had said that he had a passion for sports cars. By his driving of the Volgar he apparently also nurtured a desire to be a racing driver.

The huge car creaked and rolled on corners, slid into curbs and rocked like a seesaw as they made their way to the field, where the helicopter was housed in a small barn.

On arrival Peter jokingly made the sign of the cross on his chest, the girls smiled, then everyone followed Georges as he ran to the shed. He had certainly entered into the spirit of the chase.

To open the big doors required a great deal of physical endeavor. Then the helicopter came in to view, not a pretty sight. New paint would have been a luxury on a fuselage that appeared to have had extensive surgery, like some giant jigsaw puzzle.

"Please don't be alarmed," Georges reassured them. "There was no question of obtaining new fuselage parts, consequently I was obliged to make the repairs as best I could. It's quite safe. May I ask for some help to push it out?"

No problem. The panic was on and their anxiety to intercept Rotaru had the effect of overriding the natural precaution of the trio, who quickly overlooked the esthetic shortcomings of the helicopter. Under normal circumstances none would have agreed to fly in such a machine.

Despite its appearance the rotor began to spin on first contact. Georges calmly went through his preflight checks, then the beast lifted off. Such a helicopter is noisy by definition; in the case of this specimen there was the addition of vibration from the fuselage, consisting of many more parts than the original design had conceived and creating almost as much noise as the engine.

Georges shouted something that no one could hear, a fact that reflected in their expressions. He therefore drew their attention to the security belts. Obviously he wished them to wear the belts. They thoroughly agreed and strapped themselves in very quickly.

Slowly the helicopter lifted off and turned on to a southwesterly heading, following the road that runs parallel to the Hungarian border. The day had warmed slightly, though sitting in an ambiance supplied with fresh air at 120 mph did not give the impression that the temperature was any higher.

They were flying above the main road to Oradea and it would be south of that town where Georges expected to intercept the car.

From the information they had Rotaru had about a one-hour head start. They calculated that the Ferrari, taking into consideration the condition of the road, would be able to maintain a maximum speed of about 70 mph. The ground speed of the helicopter would be of the order of 130 mph. That being the case they would hope to have the car in sight in just over one hour.

It was one hour and ten minutes after take-off that, with the aid of binoculars, Peter began to see the car speeding down the road below. He was very upset to see his treasured Ferrari in the hands of such a person. To him it was as though it was being raped. He urged Georges to take any action that might terminate Rotaru's progress. Georges needed no encouragement; in fact he was rather more than reckless.

The moment they were near enough Georges took the rattling machine down to a position within two or three feet above the car. He then began to make arcing movements such that they arrived in a position above the bonnet and below the roof of the car. Occasionally there came the sound of metal against metal as the undercarriage of the helicopter came into contact with the hood of the car.

Suddenly Valerie's dream was brought back to mind, not only for her but also for Peter and Claudia. The only one who appeared to have forgotten the recounting of the details of the dream was Georges, who was evidently enjoying the challenge of the chase, added to which his full attention was required for the 'thickness of a hair' distance he was maintaining above the car.

Rotaru took evasive action as each swing brought the helicopter to its lowest position. Unfortunately, being more concerned with the potential impact he lost concentration on the road, for a moment, which arrived at a curve to the right. The car left the road and immediately the offside wheels entered a ditch, causing it to roll several times and throwing a considerable amount of dirt into the air, some of which found its way into the air intake of the helicopter's engine. There were several coughs from the engine and smoke began to emit from below the rotor. Once more Valerie's dream became reality.

Being so close to the ground Georges had no difficulty in setting down on the grass verge some fifty yards in front of the now still and twisted Ferrari. Poor Peter had seen his baby involved in its final move. It came to a rest on its roof, the wheels still spinning. What had been a beautiful sports car was now a mass of distorted metal.

Everyone jumped down from the helicopter and ran toward the wreck. Peter was relieved that he had taken his pistol from the glove compartment of the car the day before. He cocked it ready for action. His feeling was that he would be happy to shoot the two of them. The Ferrari could not avenge itself for having been misused.

The distance from the helicopter to the wrecked car involved just sufficient time for Peter to reconsider. His anger was tempered. The damage was done and killing was not the answer.

He led the other three and was the first to invert himself so as to look into the upturned car.

The driver and passenger remained quite still, probably dead, Peter thought, from the amount of blood splattered on the windshield and dashboard.

They decided that between the four of them they would probably be able to turn the car upright, making it much easier to extract the bodies. Should some vehicle pass they would hope to be able to send a message to the nearest hospital and police station, following which it would just be a question of time before the whole matter would be resolved.

Re-establishing the Ferrari onto its wheels was not so difficult and soon they were dragging at the door that was least damaged. It opened and they carefully eased out the body of the passenger, who appeared to have sustained serious head injuries. He also had a badly crushed leg, with the bone evident in several places through the ripped material of his trousers. If he was unconscious, rather than dead as they suspected, he was fortunate because the leg would certainly be very painful.

Having laid the passenger on the grass they went around the car to the driver's side. Rotaru was motionless. This time the door was far more difficult to open and Peter was obliged to replace the pistol in his jacket pocket so that he might have both hands free to assist. When the door did open, their first impression was that Rotaru was dead. He remained still, in a position with his head slumped down. Peter reached in and gently lifted Rotaru's head. His arms were underneath his head and unfortunately for our quartet, Rotaru had across his lap a very businesslike-looking weapon, something halfway between a revolver and an assault rifle.

He had not been injured at all, something for which they were not prepared, and the rescue and arrest situation quickly became one of Rotaru ordering them back from the car while he stepped out.

Everyone had been concentrating on the job in hand and now were frustrated at the ridiculous change of roles. They hadn't even noticed the arrival of a farmer, who had been working in a field on the opposite side of the road, though they quickly became aware of him when Rotaru began shouting at him.

Rotaru took out his identification and showed it to the farmer, who was probably illiterate, although he tried to look intelligent, studying the document very carefully. Having satisfied himself that everything was in order he moved to attention, apparently placing himself at the disposal of Rotaru, who then shouted some instructions, which meant nothing to the non-Rumanian contingent until the farmer walked across to where they had left the passenger lying on the grass. He knelt beside the lifeless figure, then after a few seconds of observation looked back to Rotaru and shook his head in a negative manner. He then crossed to the field, where he had been working, returning after a few minutes with a horse and cart.

Rotaru shouted something to his cousin, who translated that they must all help load the injured passenger on to the cart. He also took the opportunity to explain that Rotaru had told the farmer that the four of them were foreign criminals and that he was on an important secret mission. He would confiscate the farmer's car and leave everyone else while he went for assistance.

Rotaru now reverted to English and gave his instructions. Rotaru, his colleague, who was probably dead, they were not sure, and the farmer, would ride on the cart. The other four would follow behind, where he could maintain them under observation. He continued to train his ugly weapon on them with one hand and the pistol, he had taken from Peter, in the other.

Suddenly a look of curiosity filled his face when he noticed that Valerie was carrying a white stick.

"Why are you carrying a white stick?" he said. "You are not blind." Valerie replied that although she could see outlines in bright light, that was the limitation of her vision.

"You will help her," he ordered Peter. "Maybe the responsibility will occupy your mind and prevent you from taking some stupid action that might result in your death."

The ensemble moved off along the road for a short while until they arrived at an unpaved track, which presumably led to the farm because the horse changed direction, apparently needing no encouragement.

They continued for approximately two-hundred yards, arriving in front of an old barn. There the farmer jumped down from the cart and opened the door. The structure had that neglected look that seemed to be the norm in that part of Rumania. Inside a couple of primitive farm implements stood like arthritic, old men awaiting assistance in movement and in one corner was a large pile of hay.

Rotaru stood back and ordered the four to enter the barn. Once inside he instructed them to line up in front of a stall, where they waited until the farmer reappeared carrying a coil of rope.

It was evident that they were about to be tied up, worrying enough in itself; even so the chances were that had the farmer not arrived Rotaru would have shot them instantly and their participation in the whole affair would have been terminated. Now there was at least some hope.

The farmer assisted, with enthusiasm, in the process of immobilizing them, creating a series of carefully studied knots and finally securing the rope to a large iron ring that had probably been utilized for the securing of a bull in time gone by.

Rotaru had ensured that no one had anything about their person that might be used to extricate them from their captive condition. Then as he and the farmer were about to leave Valerie called to him asking that her white stick be inserted in the rope about her waist, for the moment when they were ultimately released. Her white stick was vital to her, she said, and she felt very insecure without it.

Rotaru assumed a puzzled look for a moment then, feeling confident that the stick could in no way be useful to them, picked it up from the floor and did as she had requested.

"Well, my friends, I will leave you for a moment now while I go for the farmer's car, then I shall return to bid you farewell. You have all been a great nuisance to me; however, I cannot help but regret that such talent as you have displayed proved inadequate and will shortly result in your final moments." He smiled a satisfied look as he and the farmer left.

Maybe fifteen minutes passed before Rotaru's promised return. They could hear the engine of the car still running outside as he hurried passed them and continued on to the pile of hay in the corner. There he took a cigarette lighter from his pocket and, with a look of pleasure on his face, ignited the hay, which flashed into instant fire.

"Goodbye, goodbye," he shouted as he ran out of the barn, laughing.

They heard the car door slam and then the diminishing sound as Rotaru drove away.

Claudia and Peter were filled with terror. The flame was spreading at an alarming rate and there was no way of escape. Their hands, legs and bodies were secured in such a way that they felt incapable of freeing themselves. Valerie told them to be calm, there was hope she said.

"Quickly," she urged, "the white stick at my waist. On top, if one of you can get to it, the chrome knob, when pushed, will release the outer casing and expose a knife blade."

Peter could do nothing. He was very securely tied. However, Claudia's left hand was close enough that she had little difficulty in reaching the button. With her thumb and forefinger she was able to slide the blade out of the casing and with the handle butted against the barn wall she held the knife firm while Valerie severed the rope around her wrists. To release the other three required the minimum amount of time, which was very fortunate because the fire had developed to such an extent that they were only just able to run outside before the flames engulfed the entire building.

They stood in silence for a moment as the flames raged. Timbers came crashing down and the heat, fifty feet from the inferno, was almost unbearable. Claudia observed that, as the fire developed, she had looked up and seen how smoke was accumulating at the roof of the barn. Valerie's dream had been fulfilled in all respects. They realized that without the dream Valerie may not have thought to ask for her white stick and by now they would have been roasted, a sobering thought.

They began to turn away from the barn when they were confronted once more by the farmer, who had been standing behind them for the last few moments. He had a double barreled shotgun steadily pointing at them.

Georges asked him if he remembered the name of the secret service agent.

"Certainly," he replied.

"My name is also Rotaru. He is my cousin and has stolen a great deal of money. How do you think that he could be driving such a car? The car belongs to this Englishman," he said, pointing to Peter. "And why do you think that we would be chasing him in a helicopter, if we were the criminals. And if we *were* the criminals why would you now be standing in front of your burnt-out barn?"

The farmer looked puzzled for a moment, then began to lower the shotgun, but he was not totally convinced until Georges went on to ask him why he thought Rotaru had not called the police from the telephone at the farmhouse, a fact that Georges suggested he surely would have done had he been bona fide.

"Don't let us waste any more time. We must call police headquarters in Bucharest and notify them what has happened."

The farmer was now convinced and led the group to his house, where he showed them to the telephone. Georges lifted the receiver and realized immediately that the line was . dead. He followed the wire down and found that Rotaru had ripped it from the wall.

Georges suggested that they return to the helicopter and the Ferrari. Maybe one method of transport could be made serviceable. The farmer's old Moskvic was incapable of exceeding 45 mph and at that speed Rotaru would need nine or ten hours to reach Bucharest. From there, if not sooner, he would probably try to find some way to obtain a more efficient method of transport and continue on his way to Sofia, where he would hope to withdraw the first $1,000,000.

They hurried back to the scene of the accident. There was only one in the group who was keen to get the helicopter back in the air. He went straight to it and climbed up to the area of the rotor where he began to mentally assess the damage.

Peter knew his Ferrari probably as well as Georges knew his helicopter and began instantly to force open the trunk. From there he took a tire lever and began to ease the front offside fender clear of the wheel, after which he made a quick circuit of the car and came to the conclusion that most of the damage was to the body and the car might now be driven. Both doors were still open, from when they made the mistake of wishing to give aid to Rotaru and his injured colleague.

Peter slid into the driver's seat and turned the key. The engine sprang into life immediately and produced that wonderful Italian sports car 'purr.' Valerie and Claudia quickly climbed into the car and called Georges to join them, which he declined to do saying that he had his 'baby' to care for. He waved them on, shouting, "Go!, go!. We will meet again."

They each felt sad at leaving one who had been so helpful and kind to them but the priority was to catch Rotaru. This time they agreed they would not attempt to intercept him, only follow him at a distance, so as to keep a track on him.

The doors of the Ferrari would not close and had to be held in a semi-shut position by the passengers, in addition to which there was a substantial dent in the roof, reducing even further the limited space in the back seat for Valerie.

As the Ferrari roared off in the direction of Bucharest, Valerie began to think to herself how she longed for Roberto. He must be very concerned. They had not called him since Budapest. Thirty-six hours had passed and it would be several hours more before there would be any possibility of putting his mind at rest.

NINE

That the Ferrari should move at all was surprising to everyone; that it should achieve a speed of 90 mph was remarkable, even to Peter who had great faith in his toy.

As they proceeded toward Bucharest they began to try to agree on the colour of the Moskvic they were expecting to see very soon. It was a nondescript colour, something between dark green and dark blue, the farmer had said. That he didn't know the colour of his own car gave some indication as to how dirty it was. He had confessed that he never cleaned it.

Whatever, the infrequent traffic on the road at that distance from the capital would certainly make their task a little easier.

After travelling for approximately 50 minutes Peter eased back on the accelerator, dropping the speed to about 30 mph. A severe vibration in the steering column was giving him cause for concern. They continued at that slow pace for further ten minutes until they arrived at a filling station, some 30 miles south of Cluj. There Peter said he would fill up with gas, at the same time investigating to try to establish the cause of the problem with the steering.

"You two go to the café and have something to eat and drink, Peter suggested. "I'll look under the hood and at the front suspension to see what the problem is. I can eat and drink once we are under way."

The filling station was very active, with trucks, coaches and cars and the small café, behind the petrol pumps, was bustling, causing them to wait some time to be served.

While they waited a big man with blonde hair and blue eyes, who had heard them speaking English, introduced himself to the girls as Hans. It transpired that he was from Düsseldorf and was a TIR driver on his way to Sofia, having come from Debrecin in Hungary. He travelled the road once a fortnight and this was the first time he had encountered any English tourists.

They explained that they were not exactly tourists.

"So you are here on business?" he postulated.

"In a way," Valerie responded. They wouldn't even attempt to explain.

At that point Peter joined them. He looked worried and when Claudia mentioned his concerned look he told them they would not be able to continue in the Ferrari. Hans overheard what was being said and offered to take them to Bucharest, if they were going that way. Relief replaced anxiety on Peter's face. The three looked at each other in approval and they gratefully accepted the offer.

"I'll grab that table over there and you three join me when you've been served. Do you have Rumanian Leu?"

"No." Peter replied.

"Here, take this for the moment. It is not wise to use foreign currency in rural areas."

"Thank you."

"How about language? The boss here speaks German, no English at all." Peter confirmed that he spoke German and told the girls to go with Hans, he would bring something to them.

While they were waiting for Peter to join them Hans was giving them tips on potential problems they might encounter in Rumania,

"There are many criminals here and it can be dangerous to be alone, away from the city centers. The economy is a disaster and people are almost forced to steal to eat," he warned.

Peter arrived with coffee and rolls. He had been considering their predicament and decided it wise to give Hans some background to their situation. "Listen, girls. I think we must be frank with Hans." He had a look of reliability about him and the girls nodded in agreement. Peter went on to outline a little of what was happening and the urgency of catching up with Rotaru.

"Fine, I'm game. I've had many confrontations with the police in this country and would enjoy the possibility of being the hunter rather than the hunted."

"Let's go," Peter said, full of enthusiasm.

They had more or less finished the dreadful snack and were not at all concerned at leaving the remnants. So far on the journey there had been a wide contrast in what they had consumed, both as regards food and drink. This one had ranked near the bottom.

Shortly the huge, Volvo, 16-wheel truck was speeding down the road to Sibiu, a twisting road with small villages along the way. The passengers were amazed at the power of the vehicle which achieved 90 mph without any problem. As such they were losing nothing compared with the same maximum speed the Ferrari had been able to reach, in its wrecked state. There was also considerably more room, all four being able to ride in the driver's cabin, which Hans had set up like a living room on wheels.

"Do you know the licence plate number of the Moskvic?" Hans queried.

"Unfortunately not," replied Valerie. "We're not even sure of the colour. We haven't seen the car and the farmer, to whom it belonged, could only say that it was a dark colour and very dirty."

"That would describe most cars in Rumania," Hans chuckled.

They had been driving for about one hour when they agreed that the car, half-a-mile ahead, might be the one they were looking for.

In their new mode of transport they had a major advantage over Rotaru. He would not expect to see them at all, believing them dead. If he had seen, in his rear view mirror, a smashed Ferrari drawing close he would have put on his guard but he certainly would pay no attention to a Volvo truck.

The closer they became, the more confident they grew that it was in fact the car carrying Rotaru. There was only one occupant and the car was a Moskvic, confirmed by Hans. Also it was very dirty and dark in colour.

"Shall I ram it?" Hans asked excitedly.

"I think not, for the moment," Peter replied, "I am not even sure that it is Rotaru, the back window is so dirty. Could you pull alongside?"

"No problem," Hans retorted.

There came a discordant deep rasp as Hans sounded the horn of his massive truck, then he eased the great vehicle out alongside the car,

"It is Rotaru," Claudia shouted excitedly.

By that time the truck was slightly in front of the car and Hans gradually eased the vehicle to the right, forcing Rotaru to slow down. As he did so a squeaky noise was just audible from the horn of the Moskvic. Having assured themselves that it was Rotaru the three had moved clear of the windows, so as not to be seen. Hans said that Rotaru was waving his arms and shaking his fist angrily at him as he continued to force the car off the road until Rotaru was obliged to stop, at which point he jumped out of the car, indignant and shouting abuse.

"Leave it to me," Hans said confidently as he climbed down from his truck and walked slowly toward Rotaru. The three could not hear what was said but saw as Rotaru, full of importance, displayed his identity card, a document that had given him considerable power over the years and with which he would now make a foreigner very sorry for what he had done to such an important member of the security service. In seconds Hans had Rotaru in a nelson arm lock. He then called to the others to join him.

For Rotaru three ghosts appeared. He must have thought he was dreaming. There was no way that they could be alive. He visibly blinked and his mouth opened but nothing came out.

"Well, Colonel Rotaru," Peter taunted, "you seem surprised to see us. I am sure that even in Rumania attempted murder is a serious offence. Of course you have to add the torching of the barn, with us inside and the murder of the two policemen at Satu Mare." Then turning to the truck driver, "Well done, Hans."

"Shall I break his neck?" Hans asked in pleasurable anticipation.

"I think that would not be a good idea. Do you have any rope?" Peter replied to Hans's offer.

"Sure, if you look inside that box under the chassis you will find just what we need for this heap of shit." They could not argue with the less than eloquent description.

In the box Peter found a coil of plastic coated wire which, while Hans continued to hold Rotaru, he utilized to tie his hands firmly.

"Here give that to me." Hans took the wire from Peter and made a slip-knot around Rotaru's neck, such that with any movement the loop would be tightened.

"That will keep him still," Hans said confidently, then went to a side entry door of the truck, opened it and called to Peter to bring their prisoner.

"Now we will make you comfortable for the remainder of the journey," Hans said sarcastically as he anchored Rotaru to one of the side members of the body of the truck. That being done he jumped down, looking very pleased with himself, and clapped his hands together, signifying the completion of a job well done and inquired, "Where to now?"

"That's the next problem we must consider before our arrival in Bucharest," Peter replied. "But are you sure Rotaru won't strangle himself?"

"Yes, I'm sure. I reconsidered, when I tied him to the inside of the truck, and took the loop from his neck."

The Volvo settled down to a more modest pace of between 70 and 80 mph and Peter began to fill Hans in on the details of what had happened during the preceding two days.

Hans was impressed and fascinated at what he heard and asked if they were all secret service agents. They explained that they were not. They had gradually been drawn into events like being sucked into a whirlpool. They had had no choice.

The journey continued with stories from Hans of his experiences on the road, although what he had considered to have been dramatic encounters and strange events no longer seemed that way to him. Even so the trio were pleased to hear something different for a while.

At Brasov they stopped for a dinner that proved most enjoyable, having the advantage of being with someone who knew where to go and what to order. Hans told them that one thing he always ordered in Rumania for dessert was Profiteroles and suggested that they also try them.

The advice proved sound. Everyone agreed that they had never enjoyed them so much before. Each plate had perhaps twelve of the whipped-cream-filled, small, choux pastry balls heaped into a pyramid, with hot, dark chocolate poured over the top.

Peter offered Hans a $50 bill which he declined to accept, saying he had not had such good fun for a long time. He was too big to argue with and all they could do was to thank him for the snack at the filling station and a very good dinner.

As they recommenced their journey, Hans posed a question. Did anyone know for what Brasov was famous? There was silence for a moment, then Peter, feeling very pleased with himself said, "Dracula."

"That's right," Hans confirmed. "There is a castle here called Castle Bran. You should return one day for a trip and have a look over it. It's in very good condition and the stories surrounding it and the local area are fascinating."

Hans estimated it would take a little over two hours before they would reach Bucharest. The question was what to do with Rotaru when they did arrive. If they took him to a police station they might end up being arrested themselves. No doubt Rotaru had powerful friends and would be able to twist the story.

Valerie suggested that as the stolen money was the property of the Slovak government it might be a good idea to take him to the Slovak Embassy. There they would be able to explain the whole story calmly, after which it would be the problem of the Slovaks to hand Rotaru over to the Rumanian authorities. Everyone thought that a good idea and it was agreed.

Following dinner their journey took them through the Carpathian mountains. Hans remarked what a pity it was they were travelling in the dark, being unable to enjoy the countryside and the views to the mountains, then just black spiky silhouettes against the slightly less dark sky.

Repairs to the road extended their journey so that it took three hours to reach Bucharest and it was past three in the morning when Hans turned the Volvo onto the Boulevard where he knew most of the Embassies were situated.

Having traveled the full length of that road and not finding the Slovak Embassy, they decided to wake up the British Embassy to ask for assistance.

The British Embassy they had passed already, so they quickly returned to the building and rang the night bell. Much to Peter's delight the duty officer at the embassy happened to be a good friend from his university days. They had not met for many years.

The embassy had a secure room where Rotaru was taken, still cursing. Hans decided to continue on his journey and not accept the invitation to stay at the embassy overnight with the other three. Peter, Claudia and Valerie expressed their sincere thanks for the help he had given and promised to write to him telling him the final outcome of the matter.

Peter's friend understood that they were tired and agreed to wait until morning for the full details of the incident. They replaced their empty sherry glasses on the mantelshelf above the massive hearth and left the relaxing atmosphere in front of the big open fire in the reception room.

Valerie settled down in the luxurious comfort of the huge four-poster-bed, glancing slowly around the magnificent room. There were many interesting artifacts, Flemish tapestries, Russian icons etc. Where had they come from, she wondered? There was also a fine set of Wedgewood china toilet accessories and many other exquisite antiques. The symbols of centuries of stable government, there in the British Embassy that stood like an island in that mysterious country. She felt a sense of security and gradually all the excitement of the day dissolved as she became perfectly calm and her eyes closed on the historic beauty surrounding her.

As she drifted into sleep she thought of Peter and Claudia, close in each other's arms, maybe lips touching gently. This would be the perfect atmosphere to enjoy with Roberto.

Her thoughts, bridging the phase from consciousness to sleep, inspired a dream. In the dream she stood with Roberto on the platform half-way up the Eiffel tower. It was cold and the wind encouraged them to combine the heat generated within their bodies and contain it between them.

Roberto had his hands resting just below her waist where the soft flesh rose into the firm shape of her slim buttocks. Their cheeks, red from the cold, were just touching as they gazed down at the Seine and the many bridges straddling it.

They were alone, apparently no one else having the courage to face the weather. Roberto slipped one of his arms around her waist, pressed his lips to hers and kissed her long and hard. As he did so they suddenly became aware of a confused noise from the streets below. Above all car horns repeating a rhythmic phrase. Their kiss was disturbed and as they drew apart Valerie felt a compulsion to look down at her feet. There a doll-size figure, she presumed to be that of Roberto's father, lay with bulging eyes and rigid joints. Many long pins had been inserted into the figure.

She awoke in a sweat. What had it meant? She did not have to consider for long. It seemed as though her sleeping mind had some extra-sensory perception. Bratislava, the man who had attempted to assassinate the Baron, had died so. What did Zdrazil call it? Catavaric Spasm, that was it, the terror within him at the time he died was not attributable to something in the room, it was an outside force, some voodoo or witchcraft. These were subjects of which Valerie had no knowledge, then she remembered the location and the rhythmic noise in her dream, maybe it had something to do with the French farmers, who were currently holding rallies all over France, protesting the proposed farming subsidy cuts proposed by the Baron.

Some violent splinter group could have employed the skills of a mystic. She thought and thought. It was no use trying to sleep any more.

The attempted assassination of the Baron at the castle in Bratislava provided an opportunity to establish the motive. Unfortunately, before the information could be extracted from the assassin, he had died. He had been killed by a mystic, probably from France.

At nine the following morning there came a knock on the door. "Come in," Valerie called.

A very pretty and trim young girl brought in a tray with tea, orange juice and the Times newspaper. The preceding week had seemed like a lifetime and the days had been so hectic that news from the world did not enter into her day or even her thoughts.

"Thank you," Valerie said with a smile.

"Did you sleep well, madam?"

"Unfortunately not. I was perfectly comfortable but had an unpleasant dream and could not sleep afterwards."

"I am sorry. Your friends slept very well. They didn't even respond when I knocked on their door, so I left them. The consul told me that you should be left if you preferred to sleep."

"That was very thoughtful of him. Would you kindly tell the consul that I would be happy to speak to him in one hour, if that would be convenient for him."

"Certainly, madam, good morning."

Valerie jumped from the bed and went to the adjoining bathroom. The decor was all figured marble slightly darker than cream colour and the linen was embossed with the insignia of the embassy, creating an elegant ambience.

She quickly cleaned her teeth and washed her face. She never could drink before cleaning her teeth. That having been done she began to sip the orange juice and picked up the newspaper. The orange juice was perfect, not just liquid but also the chopped up flesh of the orange, exactly as she enjoyed it. She began to feel quite relaxed but her humor changed instantly when she opened the newspaper. The headlines carried a message that epitomized the success of wrong over right. Why was it always so? The headlines announced, 'BARON GRASSINA KILLED!.'

Instantly she grabbed the telephone and asked the operator to call the hospital in Bratislava. Poor Roberto, he was alone to face the tragedy. How she longed to be with him, to console him. She should not have left. The money was not sufficient justification to leave him at such a time. Better that Zdrazil had succeeded, then the two policemen from Satu Mare would still be alive, Peter's Ferrari would be in one piece, even the farmer's barn would still be standing, and what about Georges and his beloved helicopter? She hoped that he had been able to sort out the problem.

There was a ring. She picked up the phone, "Is that the hospital?"

"Yes."

"I wish to speak to Roberto Grassina, please."

"One moment." She waited. Then the operator came on the line once more. "Roberto Grassina left the hospital yesterday afternoon. I am sorry we don't know where he went. He hadn't been discharged. The doctor went to his room and found he had gone." Valerie felt that that was all the information she would get.

"Thank you, goodbye." She replaced the receiver and began to cry, the depth of her sobbing tugging at her heart. Such a fine man, she thought, a picture of him manifested itself in her mind. He was tall, with a strong frame and an intelligent, kind face. She wiped the tears from her eyes and picked up the paper once more. This time she read the article. There had been a bomb attack in Brussels. Both the Baron and his bodyguard, Karl Weider, had died instantly. Twenty-three people in all. It was the middle of the afternoon, the Baron's car had just left the European Parliament when a bomb, that had been planted in a parked car, was detonated by remote control.

Valerie told herself that she must suppress her sadness and concentrate on getting to Bratislava as soon as possible. The Baron was dead, there was nothing she could do about that now but where was Roberto? She realized she must also break the news to Claudia and Peter. It would be very hard for Claudia, especially because of what was happening.

Valerie picked up the telephone and asked to speak to the consul, "This is the consul speaking."

"Good morning, this is Valerie. Please may we meet? It is very urgent. Something terrible has happened."

"Of course. I will send my aide to your room immediately. He will bring you to my office."

In the consul's office Valerie explained the significance of the article in the Times. The consul was very sorry to hear that it was Claudia's father who had been killed. He knew, of course, of the terrible incident but did not associate the tragedy with his guests in any way.

She went on to give him a more detailed story of the theft of the international fund. Then the consul told her how Rotaru had tried to convince the security guards that he had been brought there by three British terrorists and that if they would help him to escape they would receive a substantial reward from the Rumanian government. When they declined to help him he threatened them with all sorts of terrible things, adding that there would be a complete breakdown in relations between Rumania and Britain.

When the consul was given the story he assured the security officers, having complete confidence in Peter, that it had been a ploy and just to ensure that Rotaru was contained in absolute security.

"I think we must call Peter and Claudia. They should know the situation," Valerie said, her voice trembling.

"I agree." The consul replied He called the pretty young girl and told her to go and wake the two, telling them that there had been some important development and that they should come down as soon as possible.

While they waited Valerie continued with more details of the previous five days.

The consul was staggered to hear that the three should have experienced such incredible events. He stopped Valerie and suggested it was time to advise the ambassador. Valerie could break the news of the death of the Baron to her friends and to please tender his condolences. He appreciated that they needed to get back to Bratislava quickly but thought it would be necessary to spend a little time with the ambassador before their departure to give him as much detail as possible. The whole affair was so complex and being an international incident the full details would have to be available before it would be possible to contact the Rumanian authorities.

He left and ten minutes later Peter and Claudia joined Valerie who broke the news and showed them the newspaper. Claudia broke down and Valerie called for a doctor to give her a sedative. While they waited for the doctor Peter asked to be alone with Claudia. Valerie agreed and left them together. She then called the secretary to the ambassador saying that she was now available to help give information concerning Rotaru.

The message came back that she should join the ambassador, the consul and several other members of the embassy staff in the main conference room.

The ambassador quickly understood Valerie's anxiety to return to Bratislava but felt it would be necessary to have a witness available once the matter was brought to the attention of the Rumanian authorities. He said it had been fortunate that they had not taken Rotaru to the Slovak embassy. Had that been done it could have created a very delicate diplomatic situation.

The doctor visiting Claudia gave her a strong sedative and with gentle encouragement from Peter she was able to control her feelings sufficiently for them to join Valerie in the enquiry that was in progress.

Peter knew how much the girls wanted to get to Bratislava and suggested that, as he had been involved in all aspects of the story relating to Rotaru, he would be quite happy to make himself available as the witness. There was much discussion among the embassy staff, then finally the ambassador agreed that Valerie and Claudia might return to Bratislava, although he did ask that they keep the embassy fully informed of their position at all times.

The meeting was temporarily suspended while the girls said their farewells. They declined the invitation to lunch at the embassy but were very happy to accept the offer of a special flight in the ambassador's own private aircraft.

Peter was delighted when the embassy agreed to arrange collection of his Ferrari and bring it down to Bucharest, where he might supervise the repairs.

The aircraft was prepared and Valerie and Claudia were taken to Bucharest airport for the journey to Bratislava.

Valerie now free from the enquiries, underway at the embassy, was able, once more, to concentrate her thoughts on Roberto. Where could he be?

Claudia was very sad to be separated from Peter, who had been a great support following the news of the death of her father, even so she was, like Valerie, very anxious to know what had become of Roberto.

TEN

A little after three in the afternoon the aircraft touched down in the Slovak capital, where it was surprisingly warm, even hot, for late September. Strange that there should be such a difference in temperature from Bucharest, bearing in mind that they had traveled only about 450 miles.

The Embassy had called ahead and arranged for the girls to be met and a car was waiting. Valerie and Claudia agreed it would be better if they went straight to the Embassy. Being very important witnesses in the Zdrazil affair the VB would be very anxious to interview them. That could involve even days, giving them no opportunity to try to find Roberto. Whereas at the Embassy they could, at least, commence their enquiries by telephone.

Claudia had composed herself. She knew it was important that they work together to try to find Roberto. There would be time to grieve for their father once they were reunited with her brother. For the moment all they could do was pray that he was in no danger and not suffering.

The consul made an office and a secretary, who spoke Slovak, available to them and they began by telephoning the hospital once more. Since Valerie had called earlier that morning, the VB had been to the hospital asking questions and one of the nurses said she had seen Roberto leaving the ward in a wheelchair. He was dressed and she attached no importance to it. Further enquiries had revealed that he took a taxi from the hospital and that the taxi had been called for him by hospital reception.

Valerie then called the taxi company who promised to contact the driver and tell him to call them at the Embassy later.

For the moment that was their strongest lead. If the taxi driver could tell them where he had taken Roberto, they could continue their enquiries from there.

Valerie took the opportunity, while they waited, to call her mother who was very on edge, having expected to hear from her sooner. For the moment she decided against worrying her with the details of the past week and simply told her that she had had the flu and felt too miserable to call. She was very sorry but would be home soon and in future would call every other day.

Valerie had hardly replaced the receiver when the call came from the taxi driver. It transpired that he had been expecting to hear from them and had a note from Roberto. He agreed to call at the Embassy right away.

On hearing this the girls hugged each other and became quite excited. The important thing was that Roberto had left of his own free will and could even be somewhere in Bratislava. The possibility of an early meeting created those feelings once more in Valerie, feelings she had not experienced before with anyone.

When the driver arrived he confirmed that Roberto had described Valerie and Claudia to him and had instructed that he should give the note to no one else. The VB had already contacted him but he had been very evasive, saying simply that he had dropped Roberto in front of Billa, a large store in Vienna, that being the story Roberto had told him to use for anyone other than the girls. While he explained everything he held the note in his hand and the girls were under great strain, bursting to know the contents, but being compelled to wait while the story was told and translated. Finally he handed them the note. They held it between them while they read:

> 'My dear Valerie and Claudia, I just could not stand
> being in the hospital any more. I was worried about
> you both and all I could think to do was to go to
> Brussels and try to give some support to father.
> Please come soon, I love you both. Roberto.'

The note was like an injection of morphine. They now knew where he was and had confidence that they would soon be with him.

Valerie handed the taxi driver a $100 bill which made him very excited. He instantly placed himself and his taxi at their disposal for eternity. There was much hand-shaking and thanking and they promised to call him whenever they were in Bratislava.

The next call was to the airport to arrange tickets for a flight to Brussels. Seats were available on the morning flight from Vienna, leaving at 7:20. Until that time they had no alternative but to slow down, contemplate and look forward to the next day and their meeting with Roberto.

It would appear that the ambassadors had spoken in depth concerning their activities and the girls were treated like royalty, once again beautiful rooms being allotted to them.

Throughout the previous week they had been obliged to wear the same clothes each day, a situation foreign to them both. It was, therefore, a great joy to find the luggage, they had last seen being loaded into Zdrazil's Mercedes when they arrived in Vienna, waiting in their rooms. Valerie ran to Claudia in excitement. They just could not imagine how it could be so. They just had to know how it came about and called one of the officials who promised to enquire into the matter.

The official called them back a couple of minutes later. The answer to the puzzle was that a car had arrived at the embassy with the luggage. The driver said it belonged to two English ladies who had left the country and had asked that it be taken to the British Embassy to await their return. The driver left before the staff could get any more information or even the licence place number of the car. When Bucharest called Bratislava, to notify them of the anticipated arrival of the two girls, one of the staff recognized the names and associated them with the luggage.

Valerie and Claudia agreed that Zdrazil had been like Robin Hood. His actions had been those of a criminal, even so he had done his best to ensure that they didn't suffer. They wondered what might have become of him. He had to face the consequences of his actions but he would be better situated facing those consequences back in Bratislava.

Having given them the information regarding their luggage, the official had a message. The first secretary had asked that they join him for dinner at eight o'clock that evening.

In their elegant surroundings both Valerie and Claudia wished to make the best of themselves. Now they had their luggage they could certainly do better than they had been able during the preceding week. It was nearly 6 p.m. when they separated to prepare, agreeing to meet again just before eight.

Once more alone Valerie began to contemplate the events that had completely changed her life. Major events: the regaining of her sight, being deeply in love for the first time in her life, becoming involved in two very important international incidents. One, the matter of the fund and the second, which she realized still needed to be resolved, the European Community agricultural subsidy mystery, which had so tragically resulted in the death of the Baron. There were many questions to be answered.

The dream of the previous night had given her some food for thought. It was extraordinary that she had acquired the ability to visualize situations before they occurred. The possibility that mystic forces might be behind the death of the Baron was also very intriguing. Perhaps there was some connection. Could she be inheriting psychic powers?

She decided to soak in the bath. There she could fully relax and in that condition have the possibility to analyze all the facts.

For one hour she lay immersed in the soft warm water. She studied the taps but no images formed in the condensation. For the moment she must rely on reality. At the forthcoming meeting with Roberto, she could raise the question of the possibility of the French Farmers Union being responsible for the death of his father and that they may have employed some unusual tactics to achieve that end.

Valerie and Claudia presented a magnificent spectacle as they entered the dining room. Valerie had chosen an emerald green, velvet gown which complemented her hair. The contrast of colour, reminiscent of a painting by Rembrant, sober, yet stunningly beautiful.

Claudia, with her jet black hair, wore figure-hugging white, the ultimate contrast: black and white not colours though they certainly appeared to be so, maybe because of the contrast of texture. The gown being satin and perfectly smooth, contoured only by her beautiful body, whereas her hair was a mass of waves reflecting all the colours of the Czech crystal chandeliers.

The first secretary of the Embassy stepped forward to greet them and seemed overwhelmed by what stood before him.

"Good evening, ladies. It is my honor to welcome you to the British Embassy on behalf of his excellency the ambassador, who has asked me to inform you that it will be his pleasure to join us a little later."

They both expressed their thanks for the courtesies extended them and said that they looked forward to meeting the ambassador later.

The young diplomat made no reference whatever to what had been happening, merely discussing mundane events, the weather, politics etc., etc. They discovered, during the course of their conversation, that he had only been in Bratislava for a few days and appeared to know nothing of recent events. If he did know, he was fulfilling his role as a diplomat perfectly by avoiding the subject, maybe by instruction.

Following a good minestrone soup they were about to be served the main course when the ambassador arrived. He confessed that he hadn't seen anything so beautiful in his dining room for a long time. They sat once more and the main course of venison was served.

The ambassador apologized for being obliged to pose questions relating to the period of their captivity before Peter arrived on the scene. He would have preferred to participate in a social evening with them but as they were leaving early in the morning business had to come first.

Valerie and Claudia described the circumstances of their early involvement, in the process of which Valerie discovered something that had not occurred to her before, the fact that Claudia was on the same aircraft she had realized was no coincidence; however, although Claudia had boarded at Munich, as had Valerie, her journey had begun in London. The tickets had been left for her to collect at Heathrow, arranged, she presumed, by Roberto. Now they realized that it had been Zdrazil who had made all the travel arrangements. In the case of Claudia the break of journey in Munich was simply to ensure that the girls arrived on the same flight and not because, as Claudia thought, the direct flight was full.

There had been so much going on that it was not until now, when they began to analyze the full details, that the facts came to light, another indication of the careful planning employed by Zdrazil.

The ambassador listened in amazement to the recounting of events that had occurred during the previous week and expressed relief that Valerie and Claudia were unharmed and now providing delightful and very interesting company.

At the time of Roberto's departure from the hospital, the news of the death of his father had not been published and it was clear that he probably would not have discovered the terrible fact until his arrival in Brussels. They all hoped that he would not attempt to take matters into his own hands, especially in view of his physical condition. Valerie and Claudia had not considered that possibility until this discussion with the ambassador and began to worry. The ambassador tried to reassure them by saying that surely Roberto would find it impossible to take any action on his own while in a wheelchair. He instructed the first secretary to try to contact Roberto in Brussels and if he were successful to call Valerie so that she might speak to him. He left the dining room to make the necessary enquiries.

Valerie began to be very nervous, she had tried to reach Roberto earlier but he had not been available and even though it had been confirmed that he had arrived, no one knew where he was or when he would be back

The three were sitting in sumptuous French arm chairs and drinking port after yet another fine meal when the first secretary returned, looking very pleased. He told them that, although he had not actually spoken to Roberto, he had spoken to one of the Baron's assistants who had been with Roberto during the afternoon. The funeral had been set for 3 p.m. the next day and Roberto was fully involved in the preparations. For the moment there was no indication that he was trying on his own to locate those responsible for his father's death.

The first secretary had left a message for Roberto that Valerie and Claudia would arrive in Brussels at 8:50 in the morning and had been reassured that the flight would be met and the girls taken straight to him.

The news came as a great relief to both Valerie and Claudia, they would now be able to sleep in peace.

The next day there would be a conflict of sensations for them; they would be overjoyed to be with Roberto and they would be desperately sad to attend the funeral of the Baron. The day would be one of great happiness and great sorrow.

Before retiring the girls were pleased to hear that in the morning they would be taken to Vienna in a diplomatic car, thus avoiding, once more, the possibility of being intercepted by the VB, who presumably were searching for them. The fact that they had had similar treatment when they arrived from Bucharest, in the ambassador's aircraft, was fortunate. Had they arrived on a regular flight they would surely now be undergoing extensive interrogation, with little hope of seeing Roberto for a long time.

When Valerie awoke the following morning, she felt very relieved to have had a good night's sleep, uninterrupted by dreams. There was enough to fill her mind, above all meeting Roberto after what seemed to have been years of separation. Again the tingling and warm sensation at the thought of being once more in his arms.

Five in the morning was a little early to have to be ready to leave the embassy but she was fully awake and found Claudia to be the same when they met for a quick and early breakfast. They had said goodbye to the ambassador and first secretary the night before, promising that as soon as they had any information they would relay it to the Embassy. What they had discussed the previous evening had already been faxed to Bucharest and from now on all information would be handled that way.

It was a powerful sensation crossing the Danube once more, this time in the opposite direction, their recent memories of the journey with Zdrazil still clear in their minds. On the Slovak side of the border the 'exotic' trucks they had seen one week before appeared to be in the same positions as they had been then. Once again they were ushered through without formality to the Austrian side.

The Embassy driver told them of the incredible difference in the operation of the border since the '89 revolution. Not that the Embassy in particular had experienced difficulties but previously there had always been long queues and careful control of all traffic crossing in both directions, both as regards passengers and their baggage, whereas now, as they had seen, they had not even been obliged to show their passports.

There were long lines of cars parked but they were used, diesel-engined vehicles being imported. There was a very good market for such vehicles now that petrol was so expensive in Slovakia.

Schwachat seemed very peaceful for an international airport, as it had on the occasion of their arrival. There was not the one aircraft a minute situation as at Heathrow; however, there had to be a substantial number of passengers passing through the gates where West and East Europe meet. The arrival and departure monitors listed cities in all eastern European countries, also Russia, west Europe and the USA.

There was a slight chill in the air at the early hour but the sky was already lighting up with the promise of a beautiful day. They hoped that the weather in Brussels would be equally good for the funeral.

The flight would involve approximately one hour of excited anticipation. Valerie already felt the longing for Roberto's arms to be around her and his lips on hers.

ELEVEN

The flight was again short; even so as they drew closer to Roberto each minute for Valerie seemed like an hour.

He said she had been the object of his fantasy, now fantasy could become reality. She had kissed him, had slept beside him, the time had arrived for the full expression of his love.

The seat belt was restraining her, holding her back from him. She felt as though she would happily get out and push the aircraft to arrive just a few seconds earlier.

Now that the meeting with Roberto was secure, Claudia began to speak of Peter. She had called him late the previous evening. They had both agreed, she told Valerie, that they seemed always to be calling each other from opposite ends of the world and had vowed that once the current problems were resolved they would spend more time together.

"Will you get married?"

"Well, we didn't actually mention the word but we seem to have the same wish to be together all the time. Before I met Peter I had no serious relationships. I had many friends, but after a while I found them to be shallow or insincere and stopped seeing them. With Peter it has been quite different, he is strong and confident."

"What's his profession?" Valerie inquired.

"He's a trouble-shooter for an electronics company, that's why he's always travelling. He told me last night he intends to leave the company. He has other plans which he said we will discuss when we meet."

"When he told me that I said I would give up modeling. I don't like the work; it pays well but it's not satisfying."

"That's marvelous, I am so pleased for you both. Did he say when he might be able to leave Bucharest?"

"The latest is that in a couple of days Rumania intends to extradite Zdrazil and his group back to Slovakia. Peter couldn't get any information on Rotaru but you can be sure that he is finished and will probably spend the rest of his life in some terrible prison. He has found a mechanic, he used the description genius and they have begun work on the Ferrari. He hopes to join us the day after tomorrow, then in about two weeks he will return to collect the car."

'The captain has switched on the seat belt and no smoking signs. Would passengers kindly return to their seats and extinguish all cigarettes. We will be arriving at Brussels international airport in fifteen minutes. We thank you for flying ...."

Valerie's heart began to beat so strongly, she told Claudia she thought she had a Geiger counter in place of her heart that detected the distance to Roberto, increasing in the frequency of beat as she drew nearer to him.

"I am sure that Roberto feels the same," Claudia encouraged. "I have never seen him react to anyone the way he does to you." They smiled at one another and, as the aircraft came to a halt in front of the arrival gate, hurriedly gathered their things together.

They both commented on how they remembered arriving at Vienna just over a week before. The situation was very different then, Claudia thought Valerie was blind, Valerie didn't know too much about Roberto, the Baron was still alive. So much had happened that that flight seemed to have been years ago. If only the Baron were still alive all the other events would be insignificant.

Having completed the formalities they began to look for a card with some recognizable message, amongst the assortment being banded above the heads of the waiting throng. Then suddenly Valerie's eyes seemed to be attracted by some magnetism. They moved quickly to what appeared to be a predetermined spot. There stood Roberto. She couldn't believe her eyes. It was certainly him.

"Claudia look, Roberto is there." She pointed indicating the position. "He's standing, no wheelchair." Their brisk walk increased to a run and soon they were together with him. A triangle of bodies locked in a chain-link of arms. Roberto's lips on those of Valerie, Claudia's lips on Roberto's cheek, in a mixture of happiness in their hearts and curiosity in their minds.

The first curiosity abbreviated the kiss on Roberto's lips,

"How is it possible you have no wheelchair?" Valerie asked, excitedly.

"Yes, Roby, tell us."

"Yesterday afternoon I saw father's dear friend, Doctor Fioruccio. When he saw me in a wheelchair he told me he would like to make some tests and take X-rays. It ended up with the plaster being removed and my being given this stick."

"That's wonderful," Valerie exclaimed.

"How do you feel? Is walking difficult?" Claudia queried.

"The leg is very weak and stiff but I will be having therapy and Fioruccio tells me that the cure will get me back to normal much more quickly than sitting around in a wheelchair and that suits me fine. I am so sorry," he said squeezing both their hands, "that the joy of our meeting should be so brief. Let's hurry, we must go straight to the chapel where they have taken father's casket."

The initial excitement of the meeting was quickly replaced by a more somber mood. Valerie noticed Roberto's eyes were red and that he showed signs of not having slept. Claudia was also brought down to reality. She held a handkerchief to her eyes as they walked to the car. This was the city where her father had been blown to pieces. She felt hate for the place as a result. It was not justified but it was a natural condemning of anything associated with the death of a loved one.

Anger toward those responsible for the Baron's death had not found a place in Roberto's thoughts to this point; his entire measure of passion was consumed by despair at the loss of his father. How he had died was not the criteria, the fact that he was dead was so overpowering he seemed lost, just able to cope with mundane affairs and yet being obliged to face more. At this particular moment, a moment that should be so happy, meeting the ones he loved above anything in the world, he found himself unable to fully devote his mind and soul to that joy.

Valerie took his hand and tried to absorb some of his grief. She would happily take it all, to see him once more without pain. They had witnessed one another at the peak of exhilaration and bliss, just for a brief moment, while they were the prisoners of Zdrazil. They would voluntarily return, even to that situation, just to have the Baron alive. It could not be. He was gone, a man who seemed invincible.

Her mind jumped back to her dream of the scene in the castle at Bratislava, the vision of a forthcoming tragedy that had proven fruitless. Maybe if the dream had shown her the placing of the explosive device instead, she could have prevented his death.

The funeral in Brussels was an official affair. Baron Grassina had been a very important member of the European parliament and although Roberto would have preferred to have just a quiet family funeral, he felt it necessary to satisfy the desire of his father's colleagues to pay their homage.

Following the public funeral the remains would be flown to the family estate in Florence. There the casket would join those of his ancestors in the private chapel, amid the tall pine trees.

When Valerie learned of the arrangements she asked if she might participate. She wished to be with her new friends in their hour of sorrow. Roberto was pleased that she should ask and held her gently in his arms. Then they turned their attention to Claudia who by now had fully accepted the death of her father. For twenty-four hours she had been obliged to suppress her feelings to cope with the important matters that had affected her.

Everything else would now be set aside. The three of them would give the next two days to the Baron, a mark of respect as well as a deep-felt desire to be by his side on the journey to his last resting place.

Following the funeral in Brussels, the three went directly to the airport once more, this time to take the evening flight to Florence. On arrival there, even through their grief, the splendor of the architecture of that great city rose in all its glory, seeming to them like a massive tribute to the Baron.

The car had its passage blocked many times as they passed through the centre of the city. Even at that late hour the streets were very busy, the bustle of the people seeming to lack respect. But life goes on and it would go on for those of the family who remained.

After leaving the city they continued for a further twenty minutes until they arrived at the family estate. The four-hundred-year-old building sat high on a hill, providing a magnificent vista of Florence and the surrounding countryside.

Valerie remembered the first time she had seen Roberto on the train in those terrible circumstances, she thought then he might be Italian. It transpired that the family were Italian aristocracy but had lived outside Italy for many years, since the country had collectively agreed on a socialist system that had no place for aristocracy. The attitude had weakened since the death of the man who would have been king of Italy, under different circumstances.

It was not that the family was pretentious; it was rather that, because the Baron had been elected to the European Parliament and his blood line had come to the public attention, he had, from that time, been referred to by his family title. Still the original palace constituted the family home in all its majesty. Its spirit could not be broken by politics.

The palace was a magnificent building, blending into nature's design to perfection, each tall pencil pine enhanced some part of the structure. There were many arches and towers, so typical of Italian architecture, and a garden still full of colour so late in the year. Valerie felt love for the place, everything so beautiful, so perfect.

There was adequate accommodation for the relatives who had come from many corners of the world, uncles, aunts, cousins, nephews and nieces. The Baron had had only two children. Roberto would take his place as head of the family, inheriting the many possessions and estates that had been passed down through the centuries. He would, in future, be addressed as Baron.

It was late evening that a meeting of the senior male members of the family was called in the huge dining room, surrounded by family portraits and landscapes painted by some of the most famous artists of the previous four-hundred years. They calmly discussed the fate of the head of the family and agreed that regardless of the attempts of the police to find the killer or killers, the surviving members would not rest until his death had been avenged, a decision founded on deep-rooted Italian tradition and a desire for honor. Roberto would lead the hunt and coordinate with the rest of the family.

Valerie and Claudia were excluded from this particular meeting and found themselves surrounded by many elegant ladies firing questions at them in quick order.

The ladies were curious to know about Valerie and how she had been involved in the events of the previous week. The news of Roberto's kidnapping had, somehow, been picked up by the family, despite the fact that it had been suppressed from the media at the request of the Slovak government. This was indeed a powerful family with contacts in high places.

Valerie was happy to respond to their curiosity but would have preferred to have been questioning her inquisitors about Roberto.

All the excitement helped a little to ease the pain of the real reason they had all come together and it was well after midnight when Valerie and Claudia retired for the night, both exhausted, a condition that hit them the moment they said good night and went to their rooms.

Valerie fell into a deep sleep very quickly. There were many reasons why she should not, so much had happened, but the weight of her exhaustion outweighed all other matters and the bed was very accommodating.

It was 8 a.m. the next morning that a knock on the door brought her back to Florence and the home of Roberto. A dream had transported her to Rumania, nothing ESP this time, just a reminder of how close she had come to death. The mental re-living of the rapid consumption of the barn by the hungry fire made her shudder. At the time she had not had the opportunity to digest the full implications of what had happened, one dramatic incident quickly following the last in a series that never seemed to end until she closed her eyes on the 14th-century bedroom where she now began a new day.

"Avanti," one of the few words of Italian she knew.

Much to her great delight the door was opened by Roberto in the same vermilion silk dressing gown she had seen him wearing at the hospital. He looked perfect, his walking stick seeming to add dignity to a very handsome man, though she hoped that it would not be too long before he would be able to dispose of it.

"Forgive my disturbing your rest, dearest Valerie, I know how tired you must be; however, you did express the wish to attend the service this morning. I thought I should remind you that we will be entering the chapel at 10:30." As he spoke he slowly moved closer and closer until he was beside her, his legs resting against the bed. She felt that she could sense his heart beat amplified through the frame of the bed and into her own body where their hearts then beat as one.

"After the funeral we will begin to try to discover my father's murderer. Will you help me?"

Valerie held out her hands to him.

"It is my wish, as it is yours," she said softly. "I only met your father on two occasions but I quickly gained a very good impression of him. Before I knew you had left your wheelchair I had agreed with Claudia that we would try to track down whoever committed the hideous act, beginning immediately after the funeral today. I am so happy that we may now be together. We will find the answer I am sure. I have many things to tell you after the service. When do you wish to leave?"

"If you feel up to it, I would like to return to Brussels tomorrow."

"Arras, in France, should be our destination. It is there that we will begin to come close to the killer." Once more that extraordinary sensation of hearing herself saying something that had not occurred to her, the words came out of her mouth; but she heard them as though they came from another.

It was not the moment to discuss this further phenomenon and there was not time. She decided to tell him everything on the journey. Until then she qualified her statement by saying that she had had another dream and that she would explain later.

"For the moment you must give me time to prepare. Claudia has kindly loaned me a dress and I have not yet tried it on."

"Fine, I will see you at breakfast." He stooped and kissed her gently on the forehead. She, with her right hand, stroked his thick, wavy hair, as she did so she was filled with a strong desire to pull him down onto the bed, but she restrained herself and watched him limp away until the door closed behind him.

Valerie and Claudia were of similar stature, consequently the dress fitted perfectly. It was figure-hugging, that was acceptable, but the cleavage was too much. Valerie decided to compensate by wearing a black lacy body glove underneath, with the consequent effect of masking the rise of her breasts, leaving just a hint, like two beautiful mounds in a mist, intended only for the benefit of Roberto. Black stockings and a little less make-up than usual, completed what she considered to be perfectly acceptable for such an occasion.

She had just finished preparing when Claudia arrived.

"Wow, you look fabulous, but I can see you have sobered it a little. I think you will be perfect."

"You also look beautiful. Shall we go down to breakfast?"

"Sure, but listen Val, I wanted to say that with Peter not here I feel a bit like one too many."

"Oh, Claudia, don't be silly, you and I have been through a great deal together and I very much enjoy your company. Roberto and I will have plenty of time together later. This is not the moment, we must be formal, at least until after the service. Come on, let's go down. Anyway I need you to show me the way since this house is so big."

They walked arm in arm, Claudia leading Valerie to the more cozy summer room by the pool. There they joined Roberto and had a quiet breakfast. There was little time before the ceremony would commence, and the atmosphere had already established itself.

"I thought we should eat here this morning," Roberto said with a sigh. "The rest of the family are in the main dining room. It would really be overwhelming for me, half of them I have never seen before in my life, the rest are meeting after many years and will be exchanging life stories. I am just not in the mood for it, I had enough last night. My dear girls, I am so pleased to have you here with me, I don't know how I would have faced this without you."

The breakfast proceeded with a few more short episodes of dialogue, following which Roberto proposed, "If you are both ready we may now go to the chapel. It's 10:20 and I must be there to receive everyone."

They walked around the pool and onto a gravel path leading to the chapel. As they did so Valerie recalled the noise of gravel under the wheels of the Mercedes as they arrived at Zdrazil's house in Bratislava.

In addition to the family there were to be many dignitaries at the ceremony, with the result that the chapel was unable to accommodate everyone. Chairs had been assembled on the lawn in front of the chapel and a loudspeaker erected to permit everyone to follow the service, which was to be conducted by a representative from the Vatican.

Soon they were entering the family chapel. It was dimly lit, though adequately to delicately highlight what appeared as a cathedral in miniature. Roberto had moved ahead and Valerie was so touched by the scene that she felt she must mention her feeling. She whispered to Claudia that she thought it beautiful.

As the ceremony commenced Valerie glanced around at the series of stained glass windows. The window above the altar apparently faced east because the early morning sun was already illuminating the deep colours of the crucifixion that formed the theme of the window.

Valerie felt the tears begin to run down her cheeks and she noticed that Claudia had reached a similar state of sorrow. She glanced across at Roberto. There were no tears in his eyes; he was the head of the family now and should not demonstrate his feeling. He must have the strength to bear the pain, a pain that, despite the lack of tears, was evident in his face.

The whole congregation was united in a sincere expression of sorrow in the last farewell to a very loved head of the family.

Following the proceedings a banquet was held in the great dining hall. An ancient oak table had, as its centre piece, a silver tray on short legs of equal length to the table. On the tray were figures, again in silver and other precious metals, of knights in armor, horses, game animals and birds. There were also busts, in miniature, of family members from the previous five-hundred years.

Valerie came from a fairly wealthy family. Her father died when she was only eight years old and for the next fifteen years she had lived in Switzerland with her mother, where she attended a college for young ladies to complete her education. Even with such a background the opulence exhibited at the luncheon made her realize that, what she considered luxury, for this family was quite normal.

So this was Italy proper. She had visited twice before. On the first occasion Milan and the following year Venice but on each occasion she remembered only rain, with the addition of dense fog in Milan and a cold wind in Venice. She had been very unfortunate. With Roberto it seemed that the sun always shone and each new vista had its natural beauty enhanced by the gold of that star.

She was struck by the heart of Italy. The family had sustained a great loss and bore that loss with dignity, even so their great sorrow could be read in their faces.

After only two days she began to feel perfectly at home, a sensation she had never experienced before, not in England, Switzerland or the Black Forest, where she spent the last eight months at the blind school. It was as though she had entered a new world. She could just remain there; no other place beckoned to her. It was a very deep and very sincere feeling.

Roberto had explained that in his new position, as head of the family, he had responsibilities to all the guests and would be obliged to leave her in the capable hands of Claudia, a task he envied. It transpired exactly as he had predicted and it was not until 11:30 in the evening that he was able to come to her and repeat his sorrow at having deserted her. He kissed her gently and wished her a good night.

As Valerie lay in bed contemplating the day, she concluded that, even though she had ached to be alone with Roberto, the day had been very interesting and a wonderful experience, one she would not have missed for the world. If only that experience could have been associated with something other than the funeral of the Baron.

TWELVE

The final laying to rest of the Baron liberated the eagerness of Roberto, Valerie and Claudia to begin the hunt for those responsible for his death. During their breakfast the following morning, they sat calmly and reviewed the little evidence available to them.

Considering the first attempt on his life in Bratislava there had been no logical explanation for the strange death of the gunman. In Brussels the ballistics experts had found no detonating device, a fact that had them baffled. Perhaps the explosion *had* been triggered by a medium, as suggested by Valerie. They agreed on the possibility that some paranormal force might be implicated in both incidents.

There were no other leads and it was pointless to go to Brussels without a single clue. The police were continuing their investigations in that city. If there were any developments they would be notified.

Roberto decided to gamble on the possibility that Valerie's dream may have had some foundation in reality and selected Arras as their destination. He called his secretary and instructed her to book three seats on the flight to Paris for the following evening.

The preceding week had been traumatic and very stressful for Valerie and despite her protestation that she was happy to depart and commence the hunt for the killers of the Baron immediately, Roberto decided to delay their departure by one day, insisting that she should have a day to rest and relax. With their proximity to Pisa, he felt that 24 hours would make no difference to whatever was to happen in Arras, wandering peacefully around the architectural gem would help tranquilize her. He outlined his intention to Valerie, who was enthusiastic and also excited at the thought of the coming day together.

It was all arranged; Roberto's cousin Edoardo would drive them to Pisa in the morning. He would keep Claudia company while Valerie and Roberto permitted their minds to relax, allowing only the city and each other's company to fill the hours until they reunited at the airport at 5 p.m. Roberto and the two girls would then fly to Paris the following morning, continuing on to Arras and the mystery that awaited them there.

The journey to Pisa was a typical Italian experience. An Alfa Romeo 164 sped them down the Autostrada from Florence in sumptuous comfort. Edoardo drove with great confidence and Valerie felt completely relaxed, even at the high speed he maintained.

The famous buildings, that seem to defy gravity, create a splendor that photographs, films and paintings have not been able to fully capture. There is something awe-inspiring, a special atmosphere that surrounds the marvel that constitutes one of the most beautiful and tranquil scenes one can contemplate.

They meandered hand in hand around the city, Roberto recounting the history and being pleasantly surprised by Valerie's knowledge of the subject.

After a couple of hours Roberto's leg began to ache and they decided to stop for a coffee at a bar under a sunshade. There Valerie realized that he had his arm on the table with her hand resting on it, exactly as on the train, this time, however, she sensed no fear; in fact she was filled with the same surge of desire he described having experienced before she stabbed him.

They were captivated by the romantic atmosphere. Roberto gazed into her eyes and thought he saw, reflected there, the same craving he felt. He suggested that they go to a place where they might indulge their desires. She appreciated the significance of the suggestion and agreed.

The hotel was an exquisite, elegant building that had stood the test of time, as with the more famous structures of Pisa. Under the circumstances Valerie was surprised that she had no feeling of embarrassment as they approached the reception desk. This had not been the sort of rendezvous she had participated in before and would have expected to feel uneasy.

Roberto led her to the suite reserved for honeymoon couples. As the door closed behind them, separating them from the world, the troubles, the sadness, she glanced around the room that announced in its grace a perfect taste by whoever had completed the decor.

The delicate lace curtains swayed gently in the warm breeze, the radio was on, at a low level, music from Vivaldi's 'Seasons'. The scene was set.

She removed her jacket. Beneath she wore a wisp of a white silk blouse that clung to her breasts as they rose and fell rapidly in sympathy with the beat of her heart. Roberto moved slowly toward her, this was to be the fulfillment of the dream. He passed the back of his hand over her cheek and noticed that, as he had described in the book, her cheek bones were not so pronounced as those of his sister although her long auburn hair was exactly as he had pictured it.

He slipped his arm around her waist, as he had done on the train. There was no shock at the memory, even though the act was identical. Then his lips met hers in a firm kiss that captured their whole capacity of feeling. Gone were any memories of the horror on the train. The depth of passion that lit within them had place only for the moment.

From the time she recovered her sight and a picture of him was conveyed to her brain, she had been in love with him. It seemed inconceivable to her, an intelligent woman. Never before had she allowed her heart to rule her head. At first she had continually suppressed her feelings, denied the inner belief that he was her true love.

As their lips parted she whispered that he should lie on the bed. He kissed her once more, then obeyed her instruction.

She remained still for a moment where he had left her, then raised her arms above her head in a full stretch and slowly lowered them, one hand in front, the other behind. Her left hand travelled down the front of her face then, with her fingers still extended, between her breasts, applying pressure that had the effect of stretching the delicate silk, so that her sharp nipples almost penetrated through the material. Meanwhile her left hand had moved down her back stopping at her waist. Her slim-fitting, white skirt slipped almost silently to the floor. Roberto revelled in the beauty that confronted him. She stood in black stiletto shoes, black sheer stockings and a very narrow suspender belt. The slightest pair of panties left little to his imagination.

She moved closer to him, in her almost naked state. The exhibition she had just performed had had the desired effect.

He lay in silent anticipation. She bent over him, released the buckle on his belt and lowered the zip, thus releasing the pressure on his trousers, which she removed and deposited on the floor.

The effect of the striptease was that he displayed, in full splendor, that which she had once hoped to destroy. Her heartbeat increased at the sight of it and with both hands she grasped the prize.

Roberto could remain still no longer. He placed both his hands on her, searching no place in particular, his basic desire being to contact her flesh. Above her waist remained the silk blouse which he removed in an instant. There in full glory were the beautiful mounds that had eluded him throughout the previous day, when he had been obliged to try to take his mind from the sight of them. Valerie's feelings had been well founded, the modest effect of leaving them partly displayed had probably been more effective than parading naked.

A feast of love-making began after an enforced fast dictated by circumstances. Here they were faced by the delicacies denied them from the day of meeting. Their appetites seemed insatiable, a ballet of bodies that only reached a finale when the clock on the mantelpiece struck four.

First she slowly dressed him then, while his eyes continued to digest her beauty, she slowly reversed the action of her striptease, moved to the bed once more and kissed him long and hard.

She felt no shame as they left the hotel. They were a pair, very different in appearance but perfectly matched in all other aspects. She knew that they would be together forever. What they had done was right.

Claudia and Edoardo were already waiting at the airport. They knew the city well and although it was always a pleasure to visit they had no reason to be late. Not that Valerie and Roberto were late, they arrived on the dot of five.

Claudia knew, with her feminine eye, what the glow on Valerie's cheeks indicated. She had guessed what Roberto had in mind when he arranged the day. She had walked and talked with Edoardo, who was always entertaining company. Each time a new story; climbing in the Himalayas or flying around the world solo. Even as he related his latest feat she had imagined that Roberto and Valerie were spending little time sightseeing. The thought of what they were probably doing made her long for Peter and she wondered how long it would be before they would be together once more. Previously she had always felt uncomfortable with Roberto's girl friends, when they kissed or were close; maybe it was her protective instinct from having been his eyes for so many years. This time his own eyes had chosen what she would have been happy to choose for him.

They bade farewell to Edoardo and walked through the gate to board the aircraft.

Roberto seemed to be limping less and he confirmed that his leg was healing fast. Talk of his leg brought to Valerie's memory how the white bandage, protecting his wound, contrasted with the dark skin and thick, short, curly hair that covered his muscular thighs. For a moment her mind returned to the hotel. The hair on his chest was long. She had passed her fingers through it. It slipped between her fingers like water, smooth and soft.

"Well, you two, and how was your day?" Claudia's question brought her back to the moment,

"Valerie has a good knowledge of the building techniques of our ancestors and even though she had never before visited Pisa she knew the history well. My dear sister, I have some news for you. As you know Valerie and I met just over one week ago, a very short time, even so I am very happy to tell you that the special relationship we have found together, and that I enjoyed for two years before we met, is such that we have decided to marry."

"Roby, I am so pleased and I wish you both the very best of luck and happiness. I am sure that you will be a perfect couple. Congratulations, Valerie," she put her arms around her and kissed her on the cheek.

"It is strange in life how great sadness is often contrasted, at the same moment, by great happiness," Roberto continued, in a reflective mood. "The loss of our father has been an event I could not have coped with without Valerie. Finding the girl of my dreams can't compensate but it is like an elixir. Now that I have found contentment in my love life my goal is to find father's killers."

Claudia found Valerie *simpatico*, as the Italians say, from their first meeting and felt delighted that she was now to marry her brother.

"Let's begin to consider what we will do," Roberto continued after a slight pause. "Valerie, tell us about your dream concerning Arras."

"I told you it had been a dream because there was no time to explain. I have been experiencing a most peculiar phenomenon. It has occurred on several occasions since we met. I have said things that didn't seem to originate from me. For example, when the police questioned me after the accident I didn't tell them what had happened in the carriage and said that you were my friend. Later I gave the same story to the hospital and then my mother. Each time I made the statement I had the same sensation of listening to someone else speaking and yet the words came from my mouth."

Roberto and Claudia listened with considerable interest to what Valerie had to say. They had each witnessed episodes of Valerie exhibiting exraordinary ability but there had been little oportunity to discuss the occurrences previously.

Valerie continued, "The same thing occurred when I told you Arras would bring us near to the killers. The thought had not entered my mind. I knew that Arras exists as a town in France but why I should say such a thing I cannot imagine. Also before I met Zdrazil I had the sudden feeling that I must go to Vienna and that someone's life depended on it. Just a few hours later Zdrazil gave me the air tickets and told me that if I did not go you would be killed."

"That is extraordinary. And this 'phenomenon,' you hadn't experienced it before?" Claudia queried.

"No, I have never had any interest in the subject, nor did I believe such stories when I heard them."

"Whatever the reason," Roberto retorted, "we must hope that when we arrive in Arras this strange power you appear to have inherited will give us more clues."

"There's no way I can know but I hope so. Nothing else has come to me in the meantime."

The following morning they left the hotel at 9:30 and began the drive to Arras. The weather was not good. The night had been exceptionally cold for early October, and there was a heavy frost causing the rain from the previous day to create patchy ice on the road. Roberto and Claudia had no experience of driving in northern France, consequently Valerie took the wheel, exercising extra caution in the dangerous conditions.

The hotel was near the airport consequently they were heading away from Paris. That in itself was a relief. Roberto recalled how the last time he was in the French capital he had driven twice round the city, looking for the correct exit.

They were just a couple of miles from Arras when, despite the care Valerie was taking, they became involved in a minor accident. A woman driving in front suddenly stopped at a 'T' junction. There was still some ice on the road and their car slid into the rear of the other car. Fortunately no one was hurt.

Claudia and Valerie jumped out to apologize and exchange insurance details. The other driver remained seated, waiting for them. As they drew closer to the car Valerie suddenly had a sensation of fright and when she looked into the car she saw a doll, on the back seat, that instantly brought into her mind the dream of the doll with pins inserted all over.

She remained calm, though when her eyes met those of the other driver her fright turned almost to terror. The woman's eyes were very pale blue and piercing. Valerie felt sure that this woman was the mystic behind the killing of the Baron. She was almost unable to speak, but was obliged to because Claudia didn't speak French at all. She, on the other hand, was fluent, after her schooling in Switzerland, where French was the language employed.

"I do apologize, I am afraid that I was unable to stop because of the ice on the road. I accept full responsibility for the damage. If you wish we will go with you to a body repairer and pay whatever he estimates the cost of repairs to your car will be."

"Well, it is a pity you were so close you were unable to stop. I appreciate the problem of the ice and accept your offer. Firstly though I have to go to a meeting which will involve perhaps half an hour. Would that inconvenience you?"

"No, that's perfectly all right. We were going to stop in Arras for coffee and have plenty of time. Shall we follow you?"

"If you would. It's only a couple of miles. You will be able to get a coffee in the building where I have my meeting."

"Fine, we will see you in a few minutes. Are you sure you are OK? You were not injured at all?"

"No, I was wearing a seat belt and I feel perfectly all right. Let's go."

During the short period they were following the car, Valerie mentioned having seen the doll and her feeling of fear. Then the three of them read together the sign above a large building some fifty yards ahead. Valerie confirmed that it translated to mean, 'French Farmers Union.'

Valerie was not surprised when the car in front came to a stop in front of the building and this time Valerie stopped short.

Valerie, Claudia and Roberto followed the lady into the building where she spoke to a switchboard operator, then turned to Valerie and said that she had arranged for coffee to be brought to them in the room down the corridor to the right. She would join them there as soon as possible.

In the room the three spoke in whispered tones of Valerie's dream and her involuntary pronouncement that they should go to Arras. Apparently her feeling had been justified. It appeared that this woman was in fact the medium. They agreed that the FFU were probably using her to secure the outcome of any negotiations or agreements they were conducting. The problem would be to prove their beliefs.

Then the door opened and coffee was brought in by the telephonist. Valerie told the girl what had happened, concerning the accident, in response to which the girl laughed saying, jokingly, that they were lucky they hadn't tried to run from the scene of the accident.

"She would have got three dolls, stuck pins in them and you would have been in great pain."

"That's interesting. So she's some sort of mystic, is she?" Valerie asked.

"That's right. Since she started coming here the Union seem to be getting everything they want. I don't like her, in fact I'm frightened of her."

"I can understand that. Do you think we might take you for lunch and talk more?"

"Oh, I don't know if I can. Well, certainly not lunch time, I am meeting my boy friend." The girl was simply dressed and evidently came from a poor home. Valerie therefore took a chance, "How about dinner this evening? We would happily pay you for your time. We are from a magazine and are doing a story about your town. You may be able to help us with some information. None of us has been to Arras before."

"Well, I suppose it would be all right. I finish work at five, will you come for me?"

"Yes, we will pick you up at five."

They finished drinking their coffee and agreed that, bearing in mind the woman's ESP, they would not attempt to question her. They would start with the girl. She could be very useful, maybe help them gain access to the union files.

Valerie suddenly interrupted their conversation. "She's coming." Fifteen seconds later the door opened and the woman returned.

"If you have finished your coffee we can go to the town center. There is a good body shop there and if you do as you say there will be no need to delay you further."

They were ready and followed the woman as she left the building, continuing on to the body shop, where a price was agreed for the work and Roberto handed over the cash to cover the bill, together with some extra for the two days she would be without the car. Then they parted and went to an hotel near by.

Once they had settled in, Claudia joined the other two in their room. There they sat and talked over the strange events of the morning.

No one was more surprised than Valerie that she had been right or that she was also able to predict when the woman would return to the room at the FFU building. The discussion continued and once they had prepared their strategy for the evening Claudia returned to her room so that she might call Peter. At the same time Valerie would call her mother and Roberto would rest his leg.

"Hello, mother, I have some news for you. Are you sitting comfortably? I met Roberto Grassina on my travels. We are going to be married." There was a long silence. "In Arras in France. We came here from Roberto's home near Florence yesterday evening." Another pause. "I think in a couple of days. I have a lot more news for you .... The embassy in Bucharest? Yes, I will call them now .... Don't worry, I will explain everything when I see you .... Yes, I know I said that last time, I promise *this* time we will have a long talk. Roberto will come with me. He's looking forward to meeting you."

The conversation continued for about forty-five minutes, during which time Roberto had fallen asleep in an armchair. His head had dropped to one side and Valerie straightened him and placed pillows either side of his head to ensure that he would not have a stiff neck when he woke.

She asked the switchboard operator to call the British Embassy in Bucharest and a few moments later the call came through. The consul explained that the VB in Bratislava were very anxious to speak to the three of them. Valerie outlined their situation very briefly and promised that she would call the VB in the morning.

At 4:45 the three met, went to the car and drove to the FFU building, arriving at 4:55. Just after five the girl came out and walked across to the car. Claudia opened the door for her and as she got in they introduced one another. The girl's name was Francois.

Valerie asked, "Since we are not familiar with the town, perhaps you could recommend a good restaurant?"

Francois suggested an old chateaux approximately ten miles from the city center. She had been there just once with her fiance, who was an instructor at a rifle range. He had been invited there by a hunting club.

On the journey they learned that the mystic's name was Madam Massenet. Francois saw her for the first time about one year before. She began calling at the FFU regularly about three weeks ago. There was a file on her held by the Union secretary, although Francois hadn't seen it.

"Francois, listen to me," Valerie said with a very serious tone, "Madam Massenet is probably responsible for the death of a very important member of the European Parliament. Somehow we must get that file. We will give you 5,000 francs if you will help."

"Well, I shouldn't, but I need the money. What if we get caught and I lose my job?"

"There's no need for you to come in, just let us have the key for a while."

"No, I think I will come with you but please promise to help me if I lose my job."

"Don't worry we will take care of you. Look here's the 5,000 francs to show you we mean what we say. We will give you more later."

"Wow, thank you."

They didn't hurry their meal. Francois had said that the cleaners left the FFU building just after midnight, so they would enter about 1 a.m.

THIRTEEN

They drove slowly and quietly into a position behind the FFU building. There were no other vehicles and they decided to leave the car in a position away from the building, hoping to give the impression that it belonged to one of the members of staff, should a police patrol pass.

There was no alarm on the rear entrance simply because nothing of value was held there. Francois unlocked the door and they went in.

"The secretary's office is on the first floor at the corner facing the town and there are big windows so we can't turn on the lights," Francois cautioned.

Unfortunately they were not equipped with a flashlight and had to try to find their way by moonlight. Fortunately it transpired that there was a full moon and a clear sky that night, a fact which did not help where temperature was concerned however.

Valerie's mind returned to Pisa. There they had been able to walk in summer clothing. How she wished that she could be there now but it was not only the temperature that made her shiver.

"Why are you trembling?" Roberto asked. "Is it because you are cold?"

"Well, I am sure we are all cold but I have a strange sensation. I don't know why, let's be as quick as possible and get out of here."

Francois opened the door to the secretary's office. It was a large room and the moonlight was just adequate to make out a picture of Lenin suspended above the desk with the big leather chair.

"That's M. Cortot's desk. He is the secretary of the Arras branch of the union." There was also a conference table in the same room. "They have their meetings there with the local farmers," Francois said, pointing to the table. "Last week there was a very big party, some of the top union bosses came from all over Europe, there were delegates from Spain, Portugal and Italy. M. Cortot was very pleased with himself. We heard after that they are going to promote him."

"Francois, where are the files from the committee meetings kept?" Valerie asked.

"There is a drawer in his desk that is always keeps locked. Look, here, you see it's locked."

Roberto stepped forward and slid his hand under the front edge of the desk.

"Here it is. I did the same thing when I kept forgetting the key to my desk. Just stick the key under the edge of the desk with scotch tape. I have since overcome the problem."

The key turned and the drawer slid open exhibiting vertical files that were bulging and in disorder. Roberto noticed that there was a list stuck on the inside of the drawer. With the aid of the cigarette lighter, provided by Francois, they were able to read off the codes.

"These are codes for a computer," Roberto whispered. "Let's switch on the computer and see what they mean."

As the screen of the monitor began to light up the room, Roberto turned down the brightness to a level where they were just able to see the images. He selected the first directory code and flipped through the files quickly. They appeared to relate to the central planning of the sharing of heavy farm machinery and other farming matters.

The next file was more interesting. It was the day-to-day balance sheet. Roberto selected a date ten days back and began to slowly scan through the daily expenses until he arrived at the entries for the previous day. There was a payment in cash of 500,000 francs to Madam Massenet.

"Here it is," he said excitedly

In brackets, beside the entry, were the letters SK. There could be no doubt that it related to the killing of the assassin in Bratislava.

Roberto decided to copy the files from the computer hard drive onto a disc. Having controlled the material on the floppy disc, already in the slot, and satisfying himself that there was nothing of any use to them stored there, he began copying the files that might be useful.

He had only copied four files when Claudia whispered that there was a car moving slowly past the building. They moved to the window, keeping low and saw that the car was that of Madam Massenet. As they realized whose car it was Roberto felt a very sharp pain in his chest, then another in his stomach. Quickly he became doubled up with pain.

Valerie and Claudia immediately realized what was happening. Massenet had a doll and was sticking pins in it with the resultant pain that Roberto was experiencing. Valerie closed her eyes and tensed her body, willing the pain to stop. After a couple of minutes she felt a slight stabbing sensation in her chest, then stomach, then the pain was gone from them both. The question now was would Valerie be able to protect each one of them? She didn't know the secrets of psychics and sooner or later Madam Massenet might be able to inflict some severe injury on one of them or even kill them. There was no doubt she had the ability.

Now that Roberto was free of the pain he quickly returned to the computer and finished copying the files. He then switched off the unit and they began making their way to the back entrance. As they reached the top of the stairs they were startled by a tremendous explosion and a flash that lit up the entire building.

"Madam Massenet is busy," Claudia exclaimed.

They continued, full of apprehension, down the stairs and along the corridor.

On opening the back door they were confronted with the reason for the explosion. Their car was ablaze. There came a second explosion, causing Roberto to quickly close the door. He suggested they wait for the arrival of the fire engine that would surely come very soon. The explosions must have been heard all over the city.

Francois started to cry and kept repeating, "I will lose my job. I will lose my job." Then she began shaking violently, her legs weakened and finally she slumped to the floor.

Claudia bent over the girl, then with a frighteded voice proclaimed, "My God, she's dead."

Valerie opened the door once more to allow the light from the burning car to permit them to see more clearly what had happened to the girl. Much to their horror, as the door opened, the flickering light illuminated a body with very stiff joints and bulging eyes, exactly as Zdrazil had described the body of the man who shot the Baron.

"Oh, how horrible," cried Claudia. Roberto turned her head away and asked, "Valerie, are you all right?"

"Don't worry about me but this is a terrible tragedy, the poor girl was trying to help us and ......"

The sound of a fire engine siren interrupted her lamentation. Presumably also the police would arrive shortly. The fire engine swerved into the yard and the crew jumped down, hurriedly preparing the equipment. Soon a jet of foam smothered the flames and the light of the fire died away.

One of the firemen switched on a powerful lamp and began to scan it slowly around the area. When the beam picked out the frightened four they all began waving and shouting for help, each feeling a little more secure now that they were not alone.

The fire chief jumped in his car and drove over to where they stood.

"What happened here?" he queried.

Valerie tried to explain the cause of the explosions, though the story evidently found no credence in the ears of one who lived on the strict principle that, if you can't see it, it doesn't exist; however, at that moment the raucous sound of a police siren made any further dialogue impossible.

The police car arrived alongside the fire chief and four policemen came over. No, they hadn't seen another car at the front of the building, was the reply to Valerie's question.

"We did," the fire chief interjected. "Just as we arrived there was a Citröen leaving the area."

"That is the car of Madam Massenet," Valerie asserted. "She is a medium and caused the death of a girl."

"Which girl?" the police chief queried.

Valerie indicated in the direction of the floor behind them.

"There, her name is Francois. We only met her today."

"One moment, I think it is time for me to call the inspector." He walked back to his car where they could see him calling on his radio. After a moment he returned.

"What the hell happened to her!" Now he was closer and was able to see the unusual state of the body, he reacted with a mixture of authority disbelief and shock.

"That is what I was telling you about Madam Massenet. She is a very dangerous woman and has the power to kill people from hundreds of miles away. I witnessed the same symptoms in Bratislava."

"Bratislava, Bratislava, this story is becoming more and more ridiculous. You three get in the car, we will go to headquarters. For the moment I do not wish to hear any more of this nonsense." He ordered the other three policemen to stay with the body and search the building.

Arriving at the police station in the early morning brought memories of their arrival at the other police station in Rumania and all the tragedy that followed.

Valerie became very sad. What an appalling situation they were in. Somewhere was a crazy woman who would try to kill them all, she felt it. There was little possibility that the police would believe the story they were about to tell, added to which they would probably be accused of murdering that poor girl.

Yesterday had been so happy, she had reached the peak of bliss. It was not only the love-making that filled her mind, it was walking hand-in-hand with Roberto, talking to the fine people, seeing wonderful and beautiful sights. Perhaps all they would see now was the inside of a prison cell.

Once inside the police station Valerie suddenly knew that she must take the right hands of Roberto and Claudia. She didn't know why, but she knew that that was what she must do. She took their right hands and told them not to let go.

"What are you doing? Why are you standing in that strange position?" the policeman queried.

"It is necessary for me to hold their right hands. If not Madam Massenet would be able to kill them."

"This has gone too far already. You three are suspects in the murder of the young girl and will also be charged with breaking and entering the premises of the FFU. Now come with me, you will wait in this room until the inspector arrives."

Fortunately he left them together in the room, with the consequent effect that Valerie was able to continue to hold their hands.

Now they were alone, once more, Valerie began to give instructions to the other two. Yet again the words did not originate from her thoughts. Even so she made no attempt to stop or question what she said, believing that it was their only hope.

"Close your eyes and do not open them until I tell you." They closed their eyes. "Please do not question anything that I say. Now straighten your arms and legs and make the limbs stiff. Can you, Roberto?"

"No problem, that leg is more comfortable when it is stiff." There followed a pause, then Valerie began to utter strange words, "Rico dicos lama, carda intros dooley, zenfro aditolas noma Massenet."

There was silence for one minute.

"You may open your eyes now and we can release hands. Something has happened, I don't know what but for the moment I think we are safe." At that moment the door opened and a police officer entered the room.

"Good morning. My name is Inspector Frenais. According to my officers you three have been causing a lot of trouble in our quiet town. I would like you first to tell me what you consider important to the events of the last two hours and what you are doing here."

"My name is Valerie Henson. These are my friends, Baron Grassina and his sister Claudia."

"One moment, so you are Baron Grassina. I understood he had been killed in a bomb attack in Brussels."

Valerie explained that Roberto was the son of the Baron and took the title by heredity when his father died. Roberto handed over his passport as confirmation.

"Forgive me, sir, and my condolences on the death of your father."

Valerie went on, "We came to Arras to find the killer of the Baron. Apparently Madam Massenet, one of your towns-people, has the ability to kill by the power of thought. She uses a doll in the image of the victim, sticking pins in the doll with a final one to the heart." The police inspector listened with a certain amount of skepticism, as Valerie continued, "She began her evil deeds, that we know of, about one year ago when she tried to injure the Baron. Then one week ago she was responsible for the death of an assassin in Bratislava, after he failed to kill the Baron. Following the bomb attack in Brussels no detonator was found at the scene of the explosion. I believe that she was again responsible, detonating the bomb by her thought power. Tonight at the FFU she attempted to kill the son of the man she had killed in Brussels. She blew up our car behind the building and finally killed the girl, Francois, who died from Catavaric Spasm."

"What is that?" the inspector asked, by now listening with serious concentration.

"It is death induced by violent terror that causes the limbs to stiffen and the eyes to bulge. She utilized the same technique in Bratislava."

"Please continue, this is fascinating."

"It is impossible to know what other terrible acts she has committed. One moment. Valeries face assumed a strained look and her eyes stared in one direction. The she began to speak again. "I suggest you send someone to the junction of a road that is on a hill, where there are two grain storage towers. There you will find a car that has veered off the road and crashed into a tree."

"Can you not be more precise as to the location?"

"No, I am sorry."

"Excuse me one moment, I will ask my sergeant if he can identify the spot from your description." The inspector left the room.

"Valerie, where are you getting all this information from?" Claudia asked.

"I don't know, though I think it is coming from Madam Massenet. Suddenly, now that we are here, near to her, I am sensing much more than before. I cannot explain, but I feel that she will die and I will receive her powers, not that I want them and I certainly will not use them the same way she chose to."

Roberto remained quiet all this time. He appreciated that Valerie needed to handle the situation as she felt fit and being the only one who spoke French, he and Claudia were obliged to rely on her. He would like to have asked her many questions but decided not to interrupt, rather to wait for a full explanation later.

Shortly the inspector returned.

"OK, I think we have located the position you described and I have sent a car to investigate. I must be mad. I have never believed such things before but if what you say is correct it is obviously better to ensure that no one is injured and suffering."

For twenty minutes, Valerie continued to give the details of the past ten days. Then an officer entered the room and told them that a damaged car, a Citröen, had been found at the spot specified by Valerie. The woman driver was unconscious and had been taken to the hospital.

Valerie told the inspector that they had been able to extract some information from the computer at the FFU and suggested that it would be as well to collect all the files and computer records as soon as possible. Once M. Cortot learned what was going on he would surely try to destroy any incriminating evidence and it would appear that there was much available at the FFU.

With the most recent prediction by Valerie, the crashed car, the inspector had full confidence in her and was quite happy to act on anything she told him. He called his officers at the FFU and told them to collect all files and computer records from the offices, also to cordon off the area, permitting access to no one, in particular M. Cortot.

Then he arranged to have Cortot arrested.

The affair had international repercussions, consequently the inspector decided to contact Interpol. There were many facets to tie together: the death of the Baron in Brussels, the robbery of the funds from the bank in Bratislava, the death of the assassin in Bratislava, the involvement of Rotaru in Rumania and Russia and now the death of Francois. The inspector was becoming visibly quite excited probably envisaging universal fame for himself and promotion.

The next important thing to establish was the condition of Madam Massenet. The inspector invited the three to accompany him to the hospital.

FOURTEEN

At the hospital reception the inspector inquired as to the condition of Madam Massenet. The nurse checked the file and told him that the severe blow to the head, she had received in the car crash, had left her in a coma, otherwise there were no apparent injuries of any consequence. There was one thing the physician had noted on her file that was not clear. In strong light the pupils of her eyes remained fully open, giving rise to concern that there may be some loss of vision, a fact that could not be confirmed until she regained consciousness.

Valerie heard the report on her injuries and was not surprised, in fact she was sure that Madam Massenet was now totally blind. Everything was becoming clear to her, a logical explanation to all that had happened from the beginning. She considered the sequence of events.

The day that she lost her sight and Roberto gained his was almost certainly the first day that Madam Massenet had begun her devious activities directed against the Baron. Francois had said that Massenet first visited the FFU about one year ago.

It was probably on the occasion of that visit that she undertook a demonstration for the benefit of M. Cortot. She attempted to inflict blindness on the Baron by inserting pins into the eyes of a figure in his likeness.

For some reason the force was misdirected and the Baron was bypassed, the next possible recipient, because of bloodline, being Roberto. He was already blind and a switching effect took place, whereby he regained his sight and because he was at that moment dreaming of Valerie and bearing in mind that she had the same very unusual blood group, thereby forming a very strong link with Roberto and indirectly the Baron, it was she who had the misfortune of becoming blind.

A question began to formulate in Valerie's mind, one she wished to put to Roberto. Had his father been taken ill in any way on the day he regained his sight?

Valerie believed that from that day she began to absorb a little of Massenet's power each time she employed her evil force against the Baron, finally arriving at a point where, firstly, Valerie was able to deflect the force, as in the case of the pain that Roberto was suffering in the FFU office, then redirect the effect, as in the case of the moment she felt she must take the hands of both Claudia and Roberto in the police station, that being the moment that Massenet lost control of her car, almost certainly due to her being struck blind. Presumably at that moment she was in the process of attempting to inflict blindness on Roberto and Claudia.

The thoughts flashing through her mind were interrupted when the inspector invited the three of them to join him while he visited Madam Massenet.

In the lift Valerie had a further thought. At the moment of the attempted assassination in Bratislava she had been praying for the Baron. She would never know for sure but maybe without her prayer he would have been shot in the head.

As they approached the room, Valerie was pleased to note that the inspector had followed her advice and positioned an officer on guard outside the door. He had orders to restrain her should she recover and attempt to flee.

They entered the room and once more Valerie had that sensation of cold fear, though not to the same degree as on the first occasion. Her feeling was that she now had superior powers and that anything Massenet attempted she could override. The powers were almost certainly inherited from Massenet, though she could not conjecture as to why that should have happened or why she should think so. She just knew.

Soon after they entered the room the eye specialist arrived and made his examination. He confirmed what Valerie believed, that in his opinion, when Massenet recovered consciousness she would be blind. As Valerie heard the ophthalmologist speak, her mind jumped back to the hospital, one year previously, when she heard, with her mother, the same diagnosis of her own condition. She silently thanked God for the blessing of the return of her sight.

There was silence around the bed, each having their own thoughts. Roberto and Claudia were contemplating that this was the woman who had killed their father. Here in a foreign land, someone completely unknown to them had tried and condemned him in the interest of financial gain. How cruel it was.

Valerie considered all the events in her mind and concluded that the woman must die, no longer be permitted to kill or offer her services. This was a very difficult decision for Valerie, her nature being that she could not even kill a mouse. Massenet was a very evil being, how many she had killed or injured in some way or other it would be impossible to know. If she recovered consciousness she could and surely would begin again. It was Valerie's duty to put an end to her evil deeds, particularly to protect the ones she loved.

She knew what to do. No training was necessary. The method by which the result would be achieved she knew instinctively.

She clenched her fists and concentrated every part of her being on the woman in the hospital bed, then closed her eyes tightly, holding the position for a few seconds.

Massenet suddenly sat up in bed and emitted an ear-piercing scream, her eyes opened wide and began to bulge, then she slid down onto her back and her whole body stiffened and became still.

She was dead.

Valerie had used the power once and promised herself she would never use it again. It had to be done. There was no way of knowing what Massenet might do. No laws could deal with such a person. She employed methods not considered in the realms of legal constitution.

The final stage had been completed, from stopping the force to redirecting it and now creating it. Valerie felt no shame or pity for what she had done; however, she hoped that the terrible force had died with Massenet.

The effect of what had transpired in the hospital room had a profound effect on everyone present. They froze in horror at what they saw and the spine-chilling scream they had heard. For a few moments no one knew how to react; then the specialist stepped forward, tested the pulse and pronounced her dead.

The inspector asked the doctor what had been the cause of death, to which he replied that he had no idea, there would have to be an autopsy.

Valerie made the suggestion that her symptoms appeared to be those of one who had experienced a Catavaric Spasm.

"You may be correct. I have never seen the symptoms before although I have heard of one or two cases during recent years," the doctor replied, nodding his head with a look of learning.

As they returned to the police station the trio expressed their relief that Massenet was dead and the inspector agreed with them saying, "Someone with her potential would prove extremely difficult to contain and to contain in such a way as to make her harmless would be impossible. As I told you I did not believe such things were possible but in the last few hours I have observed things that, had someone else claimed to have seen them, I would have denied the possibility, confident with all my experience."

On their arrived at the police station Valerie had heard a policeman tell the inspector that the secretary of the Farm Workers Union had been brought in and was in the interview room. The inspector replied that first he wished to see the information from the computer disc that Roberto had copied. Then turning to Valerie, "We have come this far together. Perhaps you and your friends would care to follow the matter to its conclusion with me."

"Thank you, we would be very interested."

They went through to the communications room. There an officer was printing out the information from the discs. Roberto told Valerie to explain to the inspector that the information on the disc had been copied from stored files held under security codes. It was evident that the union was storing the information in a manner preventing its access by anyone other than those involved in the illegal activities.

The police had had more time to assess the information and found that in addition to the payment to Massenet, there was a file listing all the movements of the Baron, details of explosive experts and a detailed sketch of the roads and buildings around the European Parliament building in Brussels, evidence enough to link the union to the death of the Baron.

In the interview room Cortot was unable to explain why such information was needed by the Union and he was taken into custody pending a court hearing.

The police had arranged to collect all the records from the Union office. They already had a strong case against the Union for involvement in the death of the Baron and also the assassin in Bratislava. He had been killed to silence him.

The inspector thanked Valerie for their help in the matter and said that the three of them were free to return to Florence when they wished. There would be no need for depositions nor for them to make themselves available as witnesses. He had sufficient evidence already. Should there be any further questions he would contact them.

They shook hands with him in turn, then a police car took them to their hotel.

They had lost another night's sleep and were very tired: even so before retiring to bed Roberto booked tickets to Vienna. They would have to report to the VB in Bratislava to settle things finally before they could return to Florence.

The police driver told them he had been instructed to make himself available to take them to Paris Orly airport when they were ready to leave. Now the flight was booked, he agreed to pick them up at 9:30 the next morning. He left and they were finally alone.

Following a late breakfast, it was now 11:30. Claudia went to her room, Roberto and Valerie to theirs.

They had only been separated ten minutes when there came a gentle knock on Claudia's door. She presumed it to be Roberto or Valerie with some final thought. Upon opening the door she was delighted to see Peter standing there. He had flown from Bucharest early that morning and drove immediately to Arras, having obtained their hotel details from Valerie's mother.

Claudia was overjoyed to see him and suddenly felt tired no more. For several hours they exchanged news, gradually sinking more and more into the comfort of the bed as they spoke.

Then it was too much for Claudia. The arrival of Peter had a tranquilizing effect and while he was still giving her news of the latest condition of the Ferrari, she fell asleep. He covered her and lay beside her, just as contented as she.

They slept for perhaps two hours before they were disturbed by someone shaking the bed violently. Upon looking up they saw a young man standing above them, he was approximately twenty-five years old. He had an assault rifle trained on them and a very aggressive look on his face. It was quite obvious to them that he was very unhappy about something.

He muttered something in French that neither understood. Claudia did recognize one word he had used, it had been the name Francois. He was probably the boy friend of Francois. She had said that he was an instructor on weapons use. In his distressed state he could prove very unstable and Peter and Claudia found themselves in an unenviable position.

Peter tried to explain in French, he had forgotten ten years ago, that they did not understand. Then Claudia said, "Francois, oui, Madam Massenet, mort." The young man spoke very fast, giving them no possibility of understanding his reply.

Claudia thought she might be able to get the message across by mimicking the actions of a clairvoyant, moving her arms around, then pointing to herself and saying Massenet, then she dropped back on the bed and said, "Francois."

The young man appeared to understand what it was that Claudia was trying to say. That it was Madam Massenet who was responsible for the death of Francois. He lowered his weapon, his knees gave way and he collapsed to the floor in tears.

Claudia pulled a cover around herself, the nakedness that was her current state was intended only for Peter. She then climbed out of bed and Peter helped her to lift the young man on to the bed. There she held her arms around him saying, "Gendarme sano." He looked up at her. She had mistakenly used the Italian word for 'know', and through his tears he said, "Parla Italiano?"

"Si si." replied Claudia. That was a stroke of good fortune, because she was now able to explain what had happened and suggested that he should call at the police station and speak to the Inspector who had all the information.

Claudia expressed their sorrow for the death of his girl friend and said that she would call room service to bring some coffee, "Grazia," replied the young man. He then pushed the rifle under the bed, saying that he should not be carrying the weapon outside the rifle club. He had wanted to kill whoever was responsible for the death of Francois. Claudia confirmed that as Madam Massenet was already dead, his wishes had been fulfilled and he would not have to face the consequences of killing her.

"If you wish we will happily come to the police station with you. There you will be able to confirm what I have told you." He replied that there was no need, he had never liked

Madam Massenet and like Francois was also a little fearful of her.

Their sleep had been interrupted when they both desperately needed it, but they felt so sorry for the young man, all his dreams gone and the girl he loved dead. The day for him had begun like the end of the world.

The coffee didn't help. Up until the moment he came to their room he had anger in his heart and a task he wished to fulfill, knowing that whatever he did it would be his end also. That didn't matter, he simply wanted to avenge the death of the one he loved. Now all he had was his desperate sadness and it grew and grew inside him. He became so deeply depressed that Peter and Claudia began to be concerned for him, concerned that he might decide that life held nothing for him any further. Everything he had had and loved was gone. They decided to call a doctor.

With the help of the receptionist a doctor was located and he agreed to call at the room in one hour.

After ten minutes there was a knock on the door. This time it was Valerie. She didn't know that Peter had arrived and was very pleased for Claudia, who went on to explain about the young man, who continued sobbing bitterly.

Valerie went across to him, placed her hand on his shoulder and began to speak quietly. After a couple of minutes he began to relax, then raised his head and looked at Valerie. She took his hand and led him to a chair. There she sat beside him and continued to soothe him with words.

Peter and Claudia watched in amazement. They had done everything they could think of in an attempt to try to calm him, to no avail.

Since Claudia first met Valerie ten days previously she had seen her change day by day. It was quite remarkable. Shortly they were to become sisters-in-law and the future promised very interesting possibilities.

There came a further knock on the door. The doctor arrived and after a short while suggested that he take the boy with him to the hospital. He needed counseling and sedation.

The doctor left with the young man and before Claudia could ask what miracle Valerie had performed, Roberto arrived. He had been looking for Valerie, who had left while he still slept.

They all agreed there was no point in trying to sleep any more. It was now three in the afternoon. They would have an early dinner followed by a long night's sleep before the flight the following morning.

Valerie and Roberto returned to their room to prepare, agreeing to meet Peter and Claudia in the dining room at six. The 'Quartet' were together, initiating a bond that would see them through many difficult and exciting adventures in the future.

FIFTEEN

Claudia and Peter decided to take their shower together. It was time they held each other close and completed the actions of their desire.

From the moment of Peter's arrival he had been understanding. So much had happened, he could see how tired Claudia was and made no demands upon her. They had kissed and embraced, the closeness of their bodies fulfilling the need of the moment.

Claudia had been surprised at herself. Previously she would have wished to make love, deeply and passionately. Peter was always happy to oblige and derived as much pleasure as she but he was a calm man. Nothing seemed to agitate him or anger him. Not that he was incapable of a total expression of love; on the contrary he was a perfect lover.

Was this an effect that Valerie was having on her? She thought not, it was a confirmation of true love. That being with him, holding each other gently and telling one another of the occurrences of the previous two days, when they were separated, was fulfilling in itself. They both felt, and declared the fact to each other, that they were ecstatically happy together.

Roberto and Valerie were involved in a similar situation in their room. They had enjoyed sublime pleasure in the act of love-making and had also passed the previous hours together, without the necessity to go through the process of the actual act.

The moment had arrived once more. They had several hours alone and intended to derive the maximum sensations of the flesh that they could give to one another.

Both of the copulations began, ran their courses and reached the conclusion of ecstasy. Their actions had the effect of a very strong potion that relinquished them from the troubles of the previous days and allowed their minds to relax totally. Two pairs of lovers lay in perfect harmony, their minds completely free. Sleep enveloped Claudia and Peter in absolute satisfaction.

Valerie turned to Roberto, once calm was established and the passion subsided. It was time to explain her theory of the events that had affected them both and changed their lives forever.

Roberto listened, intrigued at the incredible things he was hearing and more convinced that fate had brought them together.

"I have one question," Valerie whispered in his ear.

"What is that, my darling."

"It relates to the day that you gained your sight and I lost mine. As I told you I believe that it was not a coincidence but the effect of an action of Madam Massenet that misrouted, for want of a better word. Cast your mind back to that day, which of course for you was a day of great joy. Did the happy event for you occur at the same time as a less happy event for your father? Was he taken ill? Did anything happen that you could not account for?"

Roberto's face assumed a look of pain. He was so in love with Valerie that being with her was a rapture, that like a drug flooded into his mind and overtook it. The question Valerie now posed cancelled the drug instantly and shouted in his brain that his father was dead. Never again would he sit and talk to him, play chess with him, sail with him or hear his words of wisdom.

He knew that his father would not wish him to mourn his passing with sackcloth and ashes, even so, it was just four days ago that his living body had been blown to pieces. His mind, the accumulation of a lifetime of intelligent thought and decision, cancelled. Tears began to fill Roberto's eyes and the spirit collapsed within him.

Valerie witnessed the effect of her question and wanted to bite out her tongue. She should have waited, given him the cure of time to help him with his grief.

She took him in her arms and felt him quiver with sadness.

"Forgive me, I should not have asked you now," she said, distraught and remorseful.

"No, it's not your fault." Roberto's voice sounded weak and distant. "You understand, I know," he said, "by making love to you I was not forgetting my father. It was somehow as though in the moment of death, new life might be created. I will answer you." He dried his eyes with a handkerchief and began.

"The day I regained my sight was a Friday, as you know. I was at the Blind Center. Once the other students and staff knew of my good fortune I decided to surprise my father and sister. I called Claudia and told her that she must go to Florence immediately. She was in London at the time. It was so urgent, I told her, she must charter a private jet to get her there at the earliest possible time. In answer to her persistent question of why? why? what has happened?, I

189

told her that there was a very big surprise and that it was a good surprise. I told her under no circumstances to call father, that she should add to the surprise." His eyes filled with tears and he swallowed to permit himself to continue.

"It was midday. I estimated that Claudia would arrive by early evening the next day, Saturday. Father, I knew, was home for the weekend, preparing a very important speech for Brussels. I called Munich and managed to get a seat on the flight for the following morning. I was so excited, I was going to see my father and sister for the first time, also the home that I loved for its tranquility." Roberto began to calm a little as he continued.

"When I arrived in Florence I took a taxi to the palace, my heart was beating so fast with the excesses of joy, the scenes so beautiful,. I wanted to touch each building, kiss everyone I saw, take the whole world in my arms. When I arrived and the staff saw me and realized that I had my sight they were excited and yet they were a little subdued, which I could not understand until I asked the question, where is my father? They seemed to be struck dumb. Well, I repeated, where is my father? The senior member of the household staff, Alberto, took my arm and told me not to worry, my father had been taken to the hospital. He was all right but had suffered a heart attack. The words were like a knife that entered my heart. Two thoughts battled in my mind; one, fright and sadness, the second. I must get to the hospital immediately."

"No one could possibly know how you suffered at that moment," Valerie said with understanding. "Such a clash of thoughts and feelings must have been almost unbearable."

Roberto kissed her softly on the forehead. Perhaps she could understand, she had experienced blindness.

"On arrival at the hospital, I spoke to the attending physician and explained about the miracle of my recovery and wondered whether the shock of learning what had happened to me might be detrimental to my father at that moment, perhaps being too great a joy for his weak heart to sustain. The surgeon told me that he had been a heart specialist for thirty years and had never witnessed a similar case. My father had suffered a massive heart attack, there was no doubt, but had made an instant full recovery. He was being held under observation because the case was so extraordinary. I understand your question. You wondered whether Massenet's initial strike had had any effect whatever on my father. There is the answer to your question."

"So," Valerie said, "Madam Massenet in one move gave you your sight, blinded me and caused your father to have a heart attack. I must tell you now that it was I who killed her. By the time we arrived at the hospital, where she lay blind on the bed, I had inherited all of her force which I used to put an end to her deeds."

"I knew it," Roberto said. "I was looking at you. I could almost see the beam leaving your body, the room seemed to fill with a great energy, then she screamed and was dead."

They kissed once, twice, three times,

"I am also puzzled about one thing," Roberto said, kissing her once more.

"Why was an assassin employed in Bratislava? Why didn't Massenet utilize her usual technique?"

"I believe," Valerie replied, kissing him once more, "having failed the first time, one year previously, Cortot used her only as back-up and that time she proved her ability.

Both had their questions answered and all that was left was to sleep.

Snow arrived early in Vienna. It occurred sometimes in late October, but at the beginning of the month, even though it dressed the naked trees and sad grass, it was not a welcome sight. They were not prepared for such conditions and were obliged to drive first to the city centre before carrying out their duty of calling on the VB in Bratislava.

Vienna offers much on a fine day but this visit would not be memorable for anything other than a couple of hours of shopping.

The four agreed that they would buy synthetic fur coats. As they explored the subject of fur coats and killing animals, also for meat, they came to the conclusion that they would also experiment with the possibility of becoming vegetarians. Each became more and more excited as they realized their unique compatibility. Whenever a problem arose they were able to discuss it and reach an amicable decision very quickly. There began the foundation of a very profound friendship.

They were very contented with the coats they had bought and agreed that it would be very difficult, if not impossible, to distinguish them from coats that involved the slaughter of hundreds of animals.

Chinese, that would be the first vegetarian lunch they would try.

They had arrived at the southern edge of the city in their search for the coats and found a Chinese restaurant quite nearby, not elegant but without cigarette smoke, and with a very pleasant aroma of cooking. At that moment they could not ask for more.

The meal was complemented by a superb Austrian lager and they agreed that they had not missed meat at all. So far in a few hours they had saved the lives of hundreds of animals and they felt good about it.

Back in the car they began the journey to Bratislava. Whilst waiting for lunch Valerie had called the British Embassy there and agreed that they would drive straight to the Embassy, estimating their time of arrival as about 4 p.m.. At 3:30 they crossed, once more, the bridge over the Danube that is inside the Slovak Republic, then drove the final ten minutes to the Embassy, arriving just before 4 p.m.

The ambassador took time to welcome them, and seemed genuinely pleased to have them as his guests, in addition to which he had been constantly badgered by the VB, whom he would be very glad to get off his back. He had notified them of the impending arrival of the quartet and, despite the late hour, had been asked to divert them, as soon as they arrived, directly to the headquarters of the VB. They had agreed because they were also very anxious to put the matter behind them and get back to Florence. Peter, in particular, was very curious to see the palace that he had heard so much about.

They had a reasonable rapport with the chief inspector of the VB, from their previous meeting. In the meantime they had been responsible for the tracking down and arrest of Zdrazil and the others in his group. The meeting was, consequently, very cordial and the debriefing continued for four hours; then it was agreed they would continue the following day.

At 10 a.m. the following morning they arrived looking bright and happy, which was more than could be said for the chief inspector, who had been obliged to write a report after the previous evening's interview, a task that had kept him busy until two in the morning, with the consequent effect on his humor, a fact that did not go unnoticed. Though it was a mood that did nothing to lessen the love of life itself that the two couples had found together, it merely caused them to chuckle amongst themselves occasionally.

Valerie asked to see Zdrazil and was granted a half-hour visit while the other three continued giving details to the inspector.

Valerie was taken to one of the interview rooms and five minutes later Zdrazil was brought in. He seemed to have aged considerably since the last time she had seen him, five days previously. His major problem was not facing justice, that had been the potential risk from the outset. What was concerning him, most of all, was being separated from his wife.

Sitting there with him, Valerie was already missing Roberto, after just ten minutes, consequently she could sympathize. The fact that he was responsible for the incarceration of his wife was something for which he would never forgive himself. It was a strange feeling Valerie had for him. He was certainly a criminal, but he had been a gentleman and she recalled his promise that he would defend her with his life, if necessary.

The half hour passed very quickly and she felt a little sad watching him being led away. He would probably spend the remainder of his life in prison.

Once back with the chief inspector, Valerie explained how Zdrazil had behaved throughout their capture and asked that he might be permitted to see his wife. It was little to ask after the help she had given. He agreed. Having heard the full story, his hard heart melted a little and he promised that he would arrange that they be held together thereafter.

Valerie felt very content at the result of her request, particularly bearing in mind the mood of the inspector. Then a thought occurred to her. This was the second occasion that she had been able to have a distinct effect on someone's feelings, firstly the boy friend of Francois and now with the inspector. Had the power of evil she had inherited, reverted to a power of good?

Having satisfied all the demands of the VB there was much handshaking and the distribution of slivovitz, a very powerful schnapps-like drink made from plums.

They left the police station with the feeling that they had contributed considerably in solving one of the most important crimes, from an international standpoint, in the short history of the Slovak Republic.

The evening had been reserved for yet another banquet at the Embassy. Knowing that they were to return to Italy the next day the ambassador had postponed a very important meeting so that he might be with them.

During the course of the evening the ambassador had some news for them from Arras. It had already been proven that M. Cortot had been acting entirely on his own. The FFU had no knowledge of the employment of Madam Massenet and had denounced Cortot and disassociated their body from him and his actions.

The ambassador treated them as friends and told them with all sincerity that they would always be welcome in the Embassy. Roberto's response was to invite the ambassador to visit *Il Palazzo*, which he promised to do in the summer of the following year. Their discussions continued until well into the early hours of the morning and they combined goodbyes with goodnights, as they would not meet again before they left to return to Florence.

On arrival at Florence airport Valerie once more had that strange sensation of returning home. Previously home had always meant where her mother was. Italy had become very important to her, not just because it was the home of Roberto and his sister, it was a sensation she could not explain to herself.

While clearing customs and passport control Valerie walked arm in arm with Roberto who, by now, was walking with just the trace of a limp.

They had just moved into the arrivals area when Claudia tugged at Valerie's arm saying, "Look, there is a lady waving at us, I think she is trying to attract your attention." Valerie turned in the direction indicated by Claudia and her heart jumped a beat when she saw her mother waving frantically. It was something like the surprise when Roberto was waiting at the airport in Brussels. She diverted her friends and led them to where her mother stood.

"So, darling, you will have to wait for another year to visit the Salzburg Festival," Valerie's mother remarked with a certain amount of acrimony.

"Mother, I am so pleased to see you, how did you find your way here?"

"Roberto's cousin Edoardo drove to Switzerland to pick me up when he heard that I was not very keen on flying. He drives rather fast but I felt perfectly safe with him."

There was yet another momentous occasion when the four, with Valerie's mother and Edoardo, arrived at the palace. The entire family were once more assembled.

The wedding had been fixed for the following day and when they entered the courtyard a huge banner announced not only the wedding of Roberto and Valerie but also that of Peter and Claudia. They had not told Valerie, keeping it as a surprise. On seeing the banner Valerie grabbed Claudia and hugged and kissed her on the cheek, then Peter, then took both their hands and expressed her delight at their decision. Peter said, jokingly, "Hey, you're not working some magic are you?"

"No, of course not," Valerie replied and they all burst into laughter.

There was a tremendous amount of happy confusion and Roberto remarked to Valerie that there is a saying that if there is no confusion the Italians will make it. In the background music was playing over loudspeakers and the sound of chatter and laughter gradually diminished leaving just the music, 'The Seasons' by Vivaldi. Valerie turned to Roberto, looked him long in the eyes. There would always be that exaggerated eye contact. She then put her hands on the nape of his neck and kissed him for a long, long, long, long time. The crowd applauded and all was happiness.

A Florida Thunderstorm

There had to have been some degree of agreement. Gentle, warm breezes that had moved toward the morning sun, caressing throughout their voyage the gulf seas, rose in lifting currents, became visible in billowing mighty clouds, spilled their; once vapor, then icy crystals, now water droplets, in unison on the thirsty earth below.

A waterholic banana palm guzzled the sweet nectar of life and continued its race to the sky above, unfolding a new creation of living green every third day.

Capillary conjunction of H^2O orchestrated into a mighty symphony of water.

From within we gazed, awaiting the scarce appearance of pale blue that becomes a dominant splash and finally the farewell greetings of wisps of white on the horizon as they hasten to catch the greater members of the family now long gone.

By God's design the birth continues, unpredictable by the soothsayers of meteorology who employ the most complex and technical components of modern science in their search to divine.

Herbert Edgar

VIKI Books sincerely hope you enjoyed reading **'Visions',** the first novel in a trilogy by Herbert Edgar.

The second book, entitled **'Quartet',** was published in February 1995 and the final book, **'Hrad'** (this strange and dramatic word is pronounced as written and has the meaning 'Castle' in the Czechoslovak language), will follow in the spring of 1995.

The four main characters of Visions; Valerie, Roberto, Claudia and Peter, have become united in an unusual bond of friendship and continue with their inadvertent involvement in mysteries and adventure

Many readers may have been frustrated by the weak hero, Roberto, in Visions. In the succeeding novel he reasserts himself and becomes the dominant character, leading his new bride, sister and brother-in-law through a series of dangerous and life-threatening situations.

If you would like to be advised as other books become available simply send your name, address and telephone number to:-

VIKI Books
P.O. Box 1228
INVERNESS
FL 34451-1228

Acknowledgments:

To Books-a-Million for their generous
policy toward new authors

To my good and patient wife.

Herbert Edgar   March 1995